# BLACKMAILED
# INTO THE
# ITALIAN'S BED

# BLACKMAILED INTO THE ITALIAN'S BED

BY

MIRANDA LEE

MILLS & BOON®

*Pure reading pleasure*

First published in Great Britain 2007
Large Print edition 2008
Harlequin Mills & Boon Limited,
Eton House, 18-24 Paradise Road,
Richmond, Surrey TW9 1SR

© Miranda Lee 2007

ISBN: 978 0 263 20010 2

Set in Times Roman 17¼ on 21¾ pt.
16-0108-42945

Printed and bound in Great Britain
by Antony Rowe Ltd, Chippenham, Wiltshire

# CHAPTER ONE

GINO stood at the hotel room window, his hands shoved deep in his trouser pockets, his dark gaze fixed on the city streets below.

The snarled traffic moved along at snail's pace, and the pavements were filled with office workers spilling from their buildings, all eager to get home for the weekend. Wherever home might be.

He wondered where *her* home was. And if she was married.

His heart missed a beat at this last thought. As perverse as it was, he didn't want her to be married.

But of course she would be. A girl like that. So beautiful and so intelligent. Some smart man would have snapped her up by now. It had been ten years, for pity's sake. She probably had a couple of kids as well.

His cellphone ringing sent him spinning away from the window. He glanced at his watch as he hurried over to where he'd left his phone, by the bed. Five-thirty. Hopefully it would be the detective agency and not Claudia. He didn't want to talk to Claudia right now.

'Gino Bortelli,' he answered, with only the faintest of Italian accents.

'Mr Bortelli?'

Gino almost sighed with relief at hearing a crisp male voice on the other end.

'Cliff Hanson here, from Confidential Investigations.'

'Glad to hear from you,' Gino returned, just as crisply. 'What do you have for me?'

'We believe we've located the Ms Jordan Gray you're looking for, Mr Bortelli, although it's not as uncommon a name as we'd hoped. But there's only one Ms Jordan Gray currently living in Sydney who matches the age and physical description you gave us.'

'She's not married, then?' Gino asked, trying to keep the excitement out of his voice.

'Nope. Still single. With no children. And you were right. She's a lawyer. Works for Stedley & Parkinson. It's an American-owned legal practice which has a branch here in the Sydney City Business District.'

'I know it,' Gino said, stunned by this news. He'd been in their offices this very afternoon, signing a contract. Hell, he might have walked right past her!

'Word is she's the up-and-coming star of their civil litigation section. Took on a big insurance company recently. And won.'

A wry smile spread over Gino's face. 'That'd be her.'

Jordan had absolutely hated insurance companies. Her parents had had an insurance claim rejected after their home had been virtually destroyed in a storm, with the insurance company hiding behind some loophole in the small print of their contract. Her father had tried to fight them through the legal system, and it had cost him every cent he had and some he didn't. After he'd lost his final appeal he'd died of a coronary, brought on by stress, leaving behind a destitute wife and a daughter.

'Do you have an address and home phone number for me?' he asked.

'An address. But no home phone number as yet. Lawyers like Ms Gray usually have unlisted numbers.'

'Give me the address,' Gino said, striding over to sit at the writing desk which contained everything a businessman away from home might require, including internet access.

He picked up the complimentary pen and jotted Jordan's address down on the notepad. It was an apartment in Kirribilli, one of the swish harbourside suburbs on the north side of Sydney, not far from the bridge. He ripped off the page and slipped it into his wallet.

'Does she live alone?' came his next question, his throat tightening.

'We don't know that yet, Mr Bortelli. We've only been on the job a few hours. We need a little more time to fill in the details of the lady's love-life. There's only so much we can find out via the internet and phone calls.'

'How much more time?'

'Possibly only a few hours. I'm having one of my best field operatives tail Ms Gray when she leaves work this evening. We've been able to secure a recent photo, courtesy of her driver's licence. He's currently staking out the exit to her building.'

Gino winced at this invasion of Jordan's privacy. 'Is that really necessary?'

'It is, if you want to know the lady's personal status tonight. Which you said you did.'

Yes, he did. He was booked on an early morning flight to Melbourne.

When he'd flown in to Sydney yesterday Gino had had no intention of hiring a private eye to find Jordan. But during his taxi ride from the airport to the city the memories he'd been trying to bury for the last decade had resurfaced with a vengeance.

The need to know what had become of her had overridden common sense. He hadn't been able to sleep last night with thinking about her.

By morning, his curiosity had become a compulsion. A call to a police friend in Melbourne had soon provided him with the number of a reputable Sydney investigative agency. By ten this morning he'd set in motion the search for the first-year law student he'd lived with for a few idyllic months, all those years ago.

*And supposing you find out there's no man in her life? What do you intend doing with that information?*

Gino grimaced.

*You were going to ask Claudia to marry you this weekend. You've even bought the ring. What in heaven's name are you doing, chasing* after an old flame who probably hasn't given you a second thought in years?

He reassured himself. *I just want to see her one more time. To make sure that she's happy. Nothing more.*

What could be the harm in that?

'Keep me updated every hour,' he said brusquely.

'Will do, Mr Bortelli.'

# CHAPTER TWO

JORDAN glanced up at the clock on the wall and willed the hands to get to ten to six, at which time she could reasonably excuse herself and go home.

She was attending the happy hour which the practice provided in the boardroom every Friday afternoon from five till six. It was a tradition at every branch of Stedley & Parkinson, introduced by the American partners when they'd begun their first practice in the United States forty years ago.

Employees who either didn't come—or left early—were frowned upon by the powers-that-be.

Normally Jordan didn't mind this end-of-week get-together.

But it had been a long and difficult week, both professionally and personally. Making small talk seemed beyond her today, which was why she'd taken her glass of white wine off into a corner by herself.

'Hiding, are we?'

Jordan looked up as Kerry angled her way into the same corner, carrying a tray of finger-food.

Kerry was the big boss's PA—the nicest girl in the place, and the closest Jordan had ever had to a best friend. A natural redhead, she had a pretty face, soft blue eyes, and fair skin which freckled in the Australian sun.

'I didn't feel like talking,' Jordan said, and picked up a tiny quiche-style tart from the tray. 'What's in these?'

'Spinach and mushroom. They're very nice, and not too fattening.'

Jordan popped the tart into her mouth, devouring it within seconds. 'Mmm, these are seriously yummy. I might have another.'

'Feel free. So what's the problem? Other

than Loverboy having flown off home today, leaving you alone for two whole weeks?'

Jordan winced at Kerry calling Chad 'Loverboy'. Yet it had been his office nickname from the first day he'd waltzed in, with his wide, all-American smile, film star looks and buckets of charm. There wasn't a single girl in the place who wouldn't have willingly gone out with Jack Stedley's only son and heir—Kerry included. But it had been Jordan he'd zeroed in on, Jordan whom he'd been dating for the past few months.

'Come on, you can tell me,' Kerry added in a conspiratorial whisper. 'I'm not a gossip like some of the other girls around here.'

Jordan knew this was true. One of Kerry's many good qualities was her discretion.

She'd also been round the block a few times, with one marriage and several boyfriends behind her—the last having broken up with her only recently. Yet she maintained a sense of optimism about life which Jordan admired and often envied.

Jordan looked into her friend's kind blue eyes and decided to do what she very rarely did. Confide.

'Chad asked me to marry him last night.'

'Wow!' Kerry exclaimed, before shooting Jordan a speculative look. 'So what's the problem? You should be over the moon.'

'I turned him down.'

'You *what?* Wait here,' Kerry said, and hurried off to give the food tray to one of the other girls to distribute, sweeping up a glass of champagne before rejoining Jordan, a stern look on her pretty face. 'I don't believe this. The Golden Boy asked you to marry him and you said no?'

'I didn't exactly say no,' Jordan hedged. 'But I didn't say yes, either. I said I wanted some time to think. I said I'd give him my answer when he gets back from the States.'

'But *why?* I thought you were mad about the man. Or as mad as a girl like you is ever going to get.'

'And what does *that* mean?'

'Oh…you know. You're super-intelligent, Jordan, and very self-contained. You're never going to lose your head over a man, like I do.'

Jordan sighed. Kerry was right. She wasn't the sort to lose her head over a man.

But she had once. And she'd never forgotten him.

'What is it that's bothering you?' Kerry persisted. 'It can't be the sex. You told me Chad was good in bed.'

'He is. Yes, he is,' she repeated, as though trying to convince herself that there wasn't anything missing in that department.

In truth, she wouldn't have thought anything *was* missing if it hadn't been for her relationship with Gino. Chad knew all the right moves in bed. But he simply could not make her feel what Gino had once made her feel.

No man could, Jordan suspected.

'What is it that you're not telling me?' Kerry asked gently.

Jordan sighed a resigned sigh. That was the trouble with confiding. It was like throwing a stone in a pond, causing ever-widening circles. Kerry was not going to rest now till Jordan had told her the truth, the whole truth and nothing but the truth.

Or at least a believable version.

'There was this guy once,' she began tentatively. 'An Italian. Oh, it was years ago, during my first year at uni. We lived together for a few months.'

'And?'

'Well, he...he was a hard act to follow.'

'I see. Obviously, you were madly in love with him?'

'Yes.'

'And what you feel for Chad doesn't compare?'

'No.' Not Chad, or any other boyfriend she'd had since.

'Was this Italian guy your first lover?'

'Yes. He was.' The first and by far the best.

'That explains it, then,' Kerry said, with satisfaction in her voice.

'Explains what?'

'It's impossible for a girl to completely forget her first lover. Not if he was good in bed. Which I'm presuming he was.'

'He was simply fantastic.'

'You know, Jordan, he probably wasn't as fantastic as you think he was. The memory can play tricks on us. For ages after my divorce I thought I was a fool for leaving my husband. But then I ran into him one night at a party and I realised he was nothing but a sleazebag and I was much better off without him. I'll bet your Italian boyfriend dumped you, didn't he?'

'Not exactly. I came home from uni one day to find a note saying that his father was seriously ill. He said he was sorry, but he had to go home to his family, and he wished me well in the future.'

'He didn't promise to write or anything?'

'No. And he didn't leave me a forwarding

address. I didn't realise till he'd gone how little I knew about him. He never talked about his family. Or called them. At least not whilst I was around. I guessed later that he was probably out here from Italy on a temporary working visa and never meant to stay.'

'That's another reason why you find it hard to forget him,' Kerry told her. 'He's unfinished business. Pity he had to return to Italy, otherwise you might have been able to look him up and see for yourself that he's not nearly as fantastic as you thought. If truth be told, he's probably fat and bald by now.'

'It's only been ten years, Kerry, not thirty. Besides, Italian men rarely go bald,' Jordan pointed out, recalling Gino's luxuriantly thick, wavy black hair. 'And Gino would never let himself get fat. He was right into physical fitness. He worked on a construction site during the day, and went to the gym several nights a week. He's the one who started me on the exercise kick.' Jordan jogged a couple of kilometres most mornings, and did weights three times a week.

'Worked as what on a construction site?' Kerry asked.

'A labourer.'

'A labourer?' Kerry repeated disbelievingly. 'You prefer a labourer to Chad Stedley?'

'Gino was very smart,' Jordan defended, 'and a darned good cook.'

'Well, bully for him,' Kerry said dismissively. 'Marry Chad and you can go out to dinner every night. Or hire your own personal *cordon bleu* chef. Look, I don't care if this Gino was Einstein and Casanova rolled into one! You have to move on, girl. You can't let some old flame spoil your future. And your future is becoming Mrs Chad Stedley. If you want my advice, as soon as Chad rings you tell him you've thought about it and your answer is yes, yes and triple yes!'

Jordan scooped in a deep breath, then let it out very slowly. 'I wish it were that easy.'

'It *is* that easy.'

Was it?

Jordan could see the sense of Kerry's arguments. Regardless of what she'd felt for Gino, he *was* past history. If you looked at things logically, to let her memory of him spoil what she could have with Chad was stupid.

Jordan was a lot of things. But stupid was not one of them.

'Yes, you're right,' she said firmly. 'I'm being silly. I'll do exactly as you said,' she decided, and felt instantly better.

Hadn't she read somewhere that any decision was better than no decision at all?

That was right. It was.

Kerry rolled her eyes. 'Thank goodness for small mercies. The girl has finally seen some sense. Look, everyone's starting to leave now. It's not my turn to help clean up, so how about we go have a celebratory drink together somewhere swanky? I don't fancy going home to an empty place just yet.'

'I'm not really dressed for swanky,' Jordan said. Unlike Kerry, whose red woollen wrap-around dress would look just as good in a nightclub as it did in the office.

'You can say that again,' Kerry said drily, as she gave Jordan's navy pin-striped trouser suit the once-over. 'Next time we go clothes shopping together I'm not going to listen to any more of your "I'm a lawyer, I have to dress conservatively" excuses. Still, if you take down your hair and undo a couple of buttons of that schoolmarm blouse, you just might not stick out like a sore thumb. We'll pop into the Ladies' and fix you up when we get there.'

'Get where?'

'How about the Rendezvous Bar? That's less swanky since they refurbished it.'

Jordan's top lip curled. 'It's also gaining a reputation as a pick-up joint.'

Kerry grinned. 'Yeah, I know.'

Jordan's eyebrows lifted skywards. 'You're incorrigible, do you know that?'

'Nah. More like desperate.'

'Oh, go on with you,' Jordan said. 'A girl as pretty as you will never be desperate.'

Kerry beamed. 'I do so love spending time with you, Jordan. You always make me feel good about myself. Want to go clothes shopping tomorrow?'

'Sorry. No can do. I have to work.'

'On a Saturday?'

'More like all weekend.' She still hadn't finished her closing address for the Johnson case. Not to her satisfaction, anyway.

Kerry wagged a finger at her. 'All work and no play makes Jordan a dull girl.'

'Which is why I agreed to go for a drink with you,' Jordan replied as she took her friend's free arm. 'So stop picking on me, woman, and let's get the hell out of here.'

# CHAPTER THREE

GINO clicked off the phone, amazed by what Cliff Hanson had just told him.

Apparently Jordan had left her office building at ten past six and walked with a female friend towards Wynyard Station. The man tailing her had presumed she was going to catch a train home. Instead, she and her companion had turned into the Regency Hotel and they were, at this very second, sitting in the bigger of the two hotel bars, having a drink.

The amazing part was that the Regency was where Gino himself was staying.

For the second time that day fate had placed Jordan on a path which could have crossed with his.

This time, however, he wasn't in ignorance

of the fact. Which was why he'd ordered Hanson to tell his operative to sit close to the door and keep an eye on Jordan till he could get down there.

Adrenaline coursed through Gino's veins as he swept up his wallet from the bedside table and slipped it into the breast pocket of his leather jacket. For a split second he hesitated, worried over what would happen when he confronted her after all these years.

Would she be pleased to see him? Or not?

Impossible to gauge how she might react. She'd loved him and he'd hurt her, no doubt about that.

Jordan was not a girl to easily forgive and forget. That he did know.

At the same time, their love affair had been ten years ago—a long time to nurse a broken heart or bitterness.

Gino scowled as he whirled and headed for the hotel room door. He'd cross those bridges when he came to them, because nothing short of death was going to stop him from going down there right now and talking to her.

Still, he was glad he'd had time to shower and change from the sleek Italian business suit he'd been wearing earlier today. Casual clothes were more in keeping with the Gino Jordan had once known, not the Gino he had become.

Which is what, exactly? he asked himself during the lift ride down to the ground floor.

A man who's forgotten what it's like to have fun, that's what.

A man weighed down by responsibility towards his family.

A man about to ask a girl he doesn't love to marry him.

An Italian girl.

If only he hadn't made that rash promise to his father on his deathbed.

But he had, and there was no going back.

Those last words echoed in Gino's head as he stepped from the lift and headed for the bar in question.

*No going back.*

What he'd once shared with Jordan was gone. If he was strictly honest, it had never been real. He'd been living a fantasy. A sexy Shangri-la which had disappeared the moment he'd received that call about his father's illness.

All that was left was a guilty memory, plus the ghost of pleasures past.

Tonight he would face that guilty memory and hopefully lay its ghost to rest.

A bouncer stood at the door to the bar, giving Gino a sharp look as he approached, but not barring his way inside.

The room was huge, with a dark blue carpet underfoot, disco-style lighting overhead, and a glitzy central bar. There were several different sitting areas, but most of the bar's patrons were clustered near the far left corner, where a three-piece combo was playing soul music.

Only a smattering of people were sitting at the tables in the area nearest the entrance, which was currently designated a no-smoking section.

Gino located the operative without any trouble—an innocuous-looking guy of around thirty, who'd blend into most crowds.

'She's over there,' he said, as soon as Gino sat down, nodding towards a table located on the edge of the dance floor.

As Gino stared through the faint smoke haze at the girl who'd once captured his heart he realised he probably wouldn't have recognised her if he'd walked right past her! Not with her glorious blonde hair scraped back up in that severe style, and certainly not dressed in that mannish trouser suit.

What had happened to the feminine girl he'd known?

She was thinner too, her face all angles.

Yet she was still beautiful. Beautiful and sad.

Both moved him: her beauty and her sadness.

'I'll take it from here,' he said gruffly to the operative. 'You can go home.'

'Are you absolutely sure?'

'Absolutely.'

The man shrugged, swallowed the rest of his beer, and left.

Gino sat there for some time, watching Jordan. She glanced repeatedly at a redhead in a red dress, who was dancing cheek to cheek with a tall, good-looking guy. Clearly this was the female colleague she had come here with. Also clearly, Jordan wasn't happy with being left to sit alone.

As soon as the band stopped playing the redhead returned to the table, accompanied by her dancing partner. After a brief conversation with Jordan, the redhead and the man headed for the exit, arm in arm.

When Jordan started downing her almost full glass of wine with considerable speed, obviously intending to leave also, Gino decided it was time to make his presence known.

The distance from his table to hers seemed endless, his chest growing tighter with each step. Just before he reached the table Jordan put down her empty wine glass then bent to her left, to retrieve her bag from the adjoining chair.

She actually had her back to him when he said, 'Hello, Jordan,' the words feeling thick on his tongue.

She twisted back to face him, her chin jerking upwards, her lovely blue eyes widening with surprise.

No…not surprise. Shock.

'Oh, my God!' she exclaimed. 'Gino!'

Shock, but not bitterness, he noted. Nor hatred.

Relief flooded through him.

'Yes,' he said with a warm smile. 'It's me. Gino. May I join you? Or are you here with someone?'

'Yes. No. No, not any more. I—' Jordan broke off, a puzzled frown forming on her small forehead. 'You've almost lost your Italian accent!'

Trust her to notice something like that, Gino thought ruefully, as he sat down at her table.

She'd always been an observant girl, with a mind like a steel trap.

When he'd first met her he'd not long been back from a four-year stint at the university in Rome, his Italian accent having thickened during his extended stay.

This reunion was going to be more awkward than he'd ever imagined. For how could he explain her observation without revealing just how much he'd deceived her all those years ago?

He had no option but to lie.

'I've been back in Australia for quite a while.'

'And you didn't think to look me up?' she threw at him.

'I couldn't imagine you'd want that,' he said carefully. 'I thought you'd have moved on.'

'I have,' she said, and tossed her head at him.

A very Jordan-like gesture, but it didn't have the same effect as it had when her hair was down.

'You became a lawyer, then?' he asked, pretending he didn't already know.

'Yes,' she said.

'Your mum must be very proud of you.'

'Mum passed away a few years back. Cancer.'

Another reason for her to look sad and lonely.

'I'm so sorry, Jordan. She was a nice woman.'

'She liked you, too.' She sighed, looking away for a moment, before looking back at him. 'So what are *you* doing nowadays?'

'I'm still working in the construction business,' he replied, hating himself for keeping up with the deception. But what else could he do? This wasn't going to go anywhere. It couldn't. This was just…closure.

Yet as he looked deep into her eyes—such lovely, expressive blue eyes—it didn't feel like closure. It felt as it had felt the first day he'd met her.

The temptation to try to resurrect something here was intense. So was his escalating curi-osity about her love-life. Okay, so she wasn't married. That didn't mean she didn't have a lover, or a live-in boyfriend.

'You're not married, I notice,' he remarked,

nodding towards her left hand, which was empty of rings.

'No,' she returned, after a slight hesitation.

Gino wondered what that meant. Had she been married and was now divorced?

'And you?' she countered, her eyes guarded.

'I might get around to it one day,' he said with a shrug.

'You always vowed you wouldn't marry till you were at least forty.'

'Did I?'

'You very definitely did.'

Gino decided to stop the small talk about himself and cut to the chase.

'What are you doing here alone, Jordan?'

'I wasn't alone,' she returned sharply. 'I was with a work colleague, but she ran into an old boyfriend of hers and he asked her out to dinner. They've just left.'

'You didn't mind?'

'Why should I mind? We only came in for a drink. It's high time I went home, anyway.'

'Why? It's only early. Is there someone special waiting for you at home? Boyfriend? Partner?'

Anger flared into her eyes. 'That's a very personal question, Gino. One which I don't feel inclined to answer.'

'Why not?'

Her eyes carried exasperation as she shook her head at him. 'You run into me by accident after ten years and think you have the right to question me over my personal life? If you were so interested in me, then why didn't you look me up when you came back to Australia?'

'I've been living in Melbourne,' he said, by way of an excuse.

'So? That's only a short plane trip away.'

'Would you have really wanted me to look you up, Jordan? Be honest now.'

Her face betrayed her. She *had* wanted him to. But no more than he'd wanted to himself.

'You could have written,' she said angrily. 'You knew my address. Whereas I had no idea where you were, other than in Italy.'

'I thought it better to make a clean break—leave you free to find someone more…suitable.'

She laughed. 'You were being cruel to be kind, then?'

'Something like that.'

She stared at him, her eyes still furious.

Gino had forgotten how worked up she could get when she thought someone wasn't being straight with her. Jordan had no tolerance of lies—or liars.

Gino conceded he'd dug a real hole for himself all those years ago. Not that it mattered what she thought of him. What mattered was whether she was happy or not.

The evidence of his eyes was troubling. She looked tired, and stressed, and frustrated. If she did have a live-in lover—or a boyfriend—he wasn't making her very happy.

'So there's no special man in your life right now?' he asked.

She glanced away for a second, then looked back at him. 'Not right now. Look, I—'

'Would you dance with me?' he asked, before she could bolt for the door.

The band had started up again, a bluesy number with a slow, sensual rhythm.

Jordan stared at him. But not so much with anger now. With a type of fear, as if he'd just asked someone scared of heights to step with him to the edge of a cliff.

Maybe she thought he was coming on to her.

He wasn't. He just wanted to find some way to get past her defences, to have her open up to him about her life.

She was a good dancer, he knew, but so was he. They'd loved going dancing together.

'For old times' sake,' he added, standing up and holding his hand out to her.

She stared at it for a long moment, as if it was a viper about to strike.

Finally she rose, taking off her jacket and draping it over her bag on the chair before placing her hand in his.

How soft it was, he thought as he drew her

onto the polished wooden dance floor. Soft and pale, with long, elegant fingers and exquisitely kept nails.

She'd always had a thing for painted nails, he recalled. Both fingers and toes. Her favourite colour had been scarlet, but she'd had bottles and bottles of nail polish, of every imaginable shade.

Tonight her fingernails were painted a deep cream, matching her blouse.

Now that her jacket was off, he could see she still had a lovely figure, despite being thinner: her breasts were still pert, her waist was tinier than ever, and her stomach athletically flat.

His mother would have said she didn't have good childbearing hips—the way Italian girls did—but Gino had always found Jordan's slender shape extremely attractive. He loved her tight little butt and her long slim legs, loved her blonde hair and her pale soft skin.

Naked, she looked like an angel.

'Put your arms up around my neck,' he suggested, after he swung her round to face him.

'You always were a bossy man,' she replied, but did as he wanted, her fingertips like velvet as they slid under the collar of his leather jacket and settled on the sensitive skin at the nape of his neck.

Gino swallowed when he started to respond. This was not what he'd intended when he'd asked her to dance. But he seemed powerless to stop himself from becoming excited.

Planting his hands on her hips, he kept his lower half a decent distance from hers—not an easy thing to do once she started swaying to the slow, thudding beat of the music.

His good intentions, Gino suspected, were doomed to failure.

'You are real, aren't you?' she said suddenly. 'Not some figment of my imagination.'

'I'm very real,' he said drily. Just as his arousal was.

Her head tipped charmingly to one side as she looked up at him.

'Amazing,' she murmured. 'And you're not fat at all.'

He tried not to laugh. If only she knew…

'Why would I be fat?' he asked.

'Lots of men gain weight after they turn thirty. What are you now? Thirty-five?'

'Thirty-six. You've *lost* weight.'

'A little.'

'You're still very beautiful.'

Her eyes stabbed his with reproach. 'Don't, Gino.'

'Don't what?'

'Don't sweet-talk me.'

'You used to like me sweet-talking you.'

'I used to like you doing a lot of things.'

He wished she hadn't said that. Her words were sparking memories which would have been better kept buried.

And they in turn sparked something he'd been trying to deny all day, struggled to control ever since he'd asked her to dance. Which was that he still wanted her—despite the years which had passed, despite everything. He wanted to take her upstairs to his hotel room right now and strip her of those sexless clothes, wanted to take down her hair and just take her, as he had ten years ago.

She'd been a virgin back then, a fact he hadn't realised till it was too late. Her innocence had shocked him at the time, but her passion had quickly banished any qualms.

That passion was still there: he could see it in her blazing blue eyes and flushed cheeks.

And it was still overriding his conscience.

'Some things don't change,' he growled.

'Everything changes, Gino. Nothing stays the same.'

'Is that so?'

His hands shifted, one sliding up her spine, the other downward to her tailbone, giving him the leverage to press her close.

As their bodies made more intimate contact a

wave of dark desire ripped through Gino, obliterating what little was left of his conscience.

'*This* hasn't changed, beautiful,' he whispered huskily.

# CHAPTER FOUR

JORDAN stiffened, then tried to stop dancing altogether. But he would have none of it, keeping her body jammed tight against his as he moved his hips from side to side.

Impossible to ignore his arousal.

Gino was impressively built. Her mind flashed back to the first time he'd made love to her. Or tried to. She'd never forgotten the shocked look on his face when he'd realised she was a virgin. She'd begged him not to stop, and he hadn't, his initial penetration punching a pained cry from her lips.

She'd gloried in the experience, impatient to do it again as soon as possible. Afterwards he'd run them both a bath and lain her on top of him in the warm water, caressing her body.

Then he'd dried her and carried her back to her bed, where he'd made love to her again, not stopping till she'd fallen into a deep sleep.

He'd given her tender body time to recover from his initial onslaught. Next morning, when he'd entered her, she'd welcomed him with a wild, wanton need. She'd climaxed swiftly and noisily.

After that, she'd always come whenever he was inside her.

Feeling his rock-hard flesh pressing into her stomach reminded her of how that felt: Gino being inside her.

Jordan suppressed a groan, burying her head under his chin to hide her flushed face from his eyes.

'I'm up here for the weekend,' he murmured, his lips in her hair. 'I'm staying here at this hotel.'

Jordan's head jerked back, her eyes disbelieving as she stared up into his darkly handsome face. 'You're staying here? At the Regency?'

'It is fate, is it not?'

Jordan shook her head. 'I don't believe in fate. Things are not predestined, Gino. People have free will. And choices.'

'And what would you choose, Jordan, if I asked you to come up to my room with me?'

Jordan's lips fell open. The arrogance of him! And the presumption!

But, oh…the passion. It blazed down at her from his beautiful black eyes, reminding her of his extraordinary virility and amazing sexual stamina. When they'd lived together it had been nothing for Gino to make love to her for hours on end, with only the shortest of breaks in between. He'd claimed he couldn't get enough of her, and his actions had backed up his words.

Gino had never been the first one to go to sleep. She'd been the one who usually pegged out, exhausted but happy.

'What for, exactly?' she snapped, even as she quivered inside at the thought of going up to his room with him. 'An old-times'-sake shag? Sorry, but I don't do one-night stands, Gino. I never did. You must remember that.'

'I remember *everything* about you,' he said, his voice vibrating with the most seductive emotion. 'And I'm not after a one-night stand. I want you to stay the whole weekend with me. I also want the opportunity to talk to you. To explain why I didn't come back for you all those years ago.'

Jordan's wildly galloping heart skittered to an unsteady halt. 'You…you wanted to come back for me?'

'Of course. I loved you, Jordan. Never doubt that.'

The last of Jordan's resistance began to crumble right then and there.

'Don't get me wrong,' he added. 'I don't want to talk tonight. Tonight is for us, Jordan. You and me together again, as we once were. Don't say no. Say *si. Si,* Gino. As I taught you all those years ago.'

Jordan's head whirled. That was another way she'd been different with Gino than with any other man since. The way he'd been able to make her submit to his will. Not like some whipped slave, but willingly and wantonly. She had wallowed in the role of being his woman. Wallowed in his possessiveness and his protectiveness. With him she'd always felt safe and secure, and totally, totally loved.

She'd been devastated when he left, devastated and despairing. That year she'd failed her exams and had to resit.

She hadn't had another boyfriend during her remaining years at university. Then, when she had eventually started dating again, she'd gone out with sweet, gentle men who were, perhaps, just a little weak. Men she could dominate and dump, once things got too serious.

Because she wasn't going to marry any of them. How could she, when she didn't love them?

Then Chad had come into her life. Smiling, charming, successful Chad, who'd impressed her with his intelligence and sophistication.

Sex with him was quite good.

She'd thought she loved him—till he'd proposed and she had suddenly been faced with a lifetime of sleeping with him.

If she were brutally honest, there was something irritatingly clinical about Chad's love-making—as if he was following a textbook on sex. Sometimes she faked her orgasm, so that he wouldn't ask her if she'd had one.

Gino had never asked her. He'd *known* she had.

Jordan trembled at the thought of how many times she would climax if she went up to his hotel room with him.

'Come on,' he decided for her. 'Let's go.'

Taking her arms from around his neck, he grabbed her left hand and began pulling her towards the exit.

'My things!' she protested, and indicated the table where, hopefully, her bag and jacket would still be on that chair.

They were.

He scowled as he watched her draw her jacket on. 'Why do you wear such unflattering clothes?'

Her eyes flicked over his outfit. Tight black jeans, a white T-shirt and a black leather jacket. He'd always been a jeans and T-shirt kind of guy. They suited Gino's tall, macho body.

'Female lawyers wear clothes like this to work,' she said. She didn't add, *Especially ones who looked like her.* The law was still a man's world, no matter what feminists liked to think. Even women clients preferred a male lawyer.

'You look better in a dress,' he returned, taking her elbow and steering her towards the exit. 'Or at least a skirt. You should never wear trousers, Jordan.'

Heat flooded her body as she recalled how, after Gino had been living with her for a while, he'd forbidden her to wear underwear. She'd fought him over that. At first. But he'd managed to convince her, and she'd started going round with nothing on under her clothes.

Which was why she'd worn dresses and skirts back then, and not jeans or trousers.

Oh, heavens, she felt hot, so hot.

Thankfully, the air outside the bar was much cooler. Jordan scooped in some calming breaths as Gino urged her along the marble-floored arcade which led to the hotel foyer proper. If she was going to do this she would rather do it with a clear head, not because she was mindlessly turned on.

But it was no use. She *was* mindlessly turned on.

She tried warning herself that he might have become a heartless womaniser, was just spinning her a line to get her into bed for the night.

But she wasn't convinced. He'd seemed so sincere just now. Sincere and very passionate.

At the same time Jordan was desperate to find the answers to all those questions about Gino which had plagued her for the last ten years.

He'd promised to explain everything in the morning.

Meanwhile...

It was the meanwhile which was sending her into a spin.

Was she really going to do this? Go to bed with Gino within ten minutes of running into him again?

Her heart fluttered wildly as her eyes raked over him. He was everything she remembered. And more...more handsome, more mature... and even more masterful.

She would not have believed herself capable of being seduced so quickly these days, even by Gino.

But seduce her he had, in no time flat.

Jordan knew that if she spent the night with her wickedly sexy former lover then it would be Chad who'd be history. She'd had a slim chance of forgetting Gino when he'd been safely consigned to the past. No way could she forget him now.

Still, maybe she wouldn't have to forget him

this time. Maybe they really could take up where they left off.

Oh, she hoped so.

'What are you doing up here in Sydney?' she asked, almost running to keep up with him. 'And why are you staying here? This is a very expensive hotel.'

'Don't ask questions, Jordan,' he returned, his tone impatient. 'Not right now. Leave it till the morning.'

She opened her mouth, then closed it again. In truth, she didn't want to talk. But she didn't want to think, either. And silence encouraged thinking.

Thinking brought doubts and worries. She could imagine what Kerry would think if she saw her now. She's say she was insane!

When they reached the bank of lifts, one of them was empty and waiting. Gino took no time steering her inside, inserting his key card and pressing the tenth floor. The moment the doors closed he pulled her forcefully into his arms.

'I can't wait another second,' he growled, his mouth already descending.

What was it that made one man's kiss different from another?

Jordan had once tried to analyse this when other men's kisses never did for her what Gino's had done.

Now she knew: it was not just a matter of technique, or the sensual shape of his mouth. It was the passion behind those kisses, that all-encompassing hunger which came not just from his lips and tongue, but from his whole body.

Jordan was panting by the time he wrenched his mouth away.

His black eyes blazed down at her. 'I should never have left you,' he said. 'Never!'

The lift had stopped by then, and the doors slid open. Two couples were waiting there to get in, all glammed up for a Friday night on the town. The women glanced at Gino as they exited, the men at Jordan.

She cringed a little when she saw her reflection in the mirror on the wall opposite. She looked dishevelled—some strands of hair falling down, her mouth devoid of lipstick, her eyes dilated and glittering with desires as yet unsatisfied.

Gino enfolded her hand in his and drew her along a carpeted hallway, stopping in front of room number 107.

As he bent his head to insert his key card again, Jordan noticed that his hair was shorter than he'd once worn it. She wondered if he was still a construction labourer. Maybe he was a foreman by now.

Another thought popped into her mind as he opened the door and waved her inside. Surely he must have a girlfriend back in Melbourne. Men like Gino didn't live celibate lives.

As jealous as this idea made her, Jordan held her tongue, not wanting to spoil the moment with any upsetting truths. All she needed to know for now was that he wasn't married and that he still desired her. As she still desired him.

*But do you still love him?* came the intriguing question as Gino followed her into the hotel room, kicking the door shut behind them.

Jordan was no longer a romantic teenager. She'd learned in the decade post-Gino that falling in love did not come as easily when you'd seen more of life. And of men.

When Gino curled his hands over her shoulders and leant her back against him Jordan realised she didn't care if she still loved him or not. Her desires had moved past the point of no return. She was Gino's woman again. At least for tonight. No, for the whole weekend.

An erotic shiver rippled down her spine as he eased her jacket off her shoulders.

'Do you wish to go to the bathroom first?' he whispered.

'No,' she choked out.

Her jacket gone, he turned her round and began unbuttoning her blouse. When her nipples tightened within her bra, she closed her eyes.

'Open your eyes,' he commanded.

She obeyed him, if a little reluctantly.

'Now keep them open. I want you to see that it is Gino making love to you.'

'You think I wouldn't know it was you, even with my eyes closed?'

His smile was almost smug. 'You have not forgotten me?'

'I remember everything about you, Gino,' she said, echoing his words down in the bar.

His eyes smouldered as he stripped the blouse from her body, then her bra.

'Then you will remember I am not always a patient lover.'

Jordan's mouth went dry.

Sometimes, when he'd come home from work, he'd lifted her skirt and taken her swiftly, standing up. No foreplay. Just his flesh filling hers whilst he told her how he'd thought about doing this to her all day.

His impassioned words had excited her as much as his actions, sending her over the edge within a shockingly short space of time.

She shuddered at the thought that this was what he was going to do to her now. Though he couldn't, could he? Not with what she was still wearing.

'You should not cover your beautiful body with clothes such as these,' he told her, as he unzipped her pin-striped trousers and pushed them down over her hips. When they pooled onto the floor she stepped out of them, leaving her standing there in nothing but cream cotton panties, beige knee-high stockings and sensible black pumps.

'Ridiculous,' he growled, his top lip curling at the sight of her. 'Get them off. Get everything off!'

She might have done as he ordered if he hadn't started undressing himself, tossing aside his black leather jacket and reefing the white T-shirt over his head in a flash.

The sudden baring of his chest kept her rooted to the spot, her heart thudding as her eyes washed over him. He was leaner than he had been ten years ago—leaner, yet still utterly gorgeous.

'Do you want me to do it? Is that it?' he asked as he unzipped his jeans and shoved them down, taking his underpants with them.

Jordan swallowed. 'What?'

Gino shot her a frustrated glance before sitting down on the edge of the bed and yanking off his shoes and socks.

Once totally naked, he remained sitting there, his dark eyes narrowing as they travelled up and down her tautly held body.

'You *are* thinner,' he said.

'So are you,' she countered, desperate to find some strength to fight the wave of weakness which was washing through her. 'And your hair's shorter.'

'Is yours?'

'No.'

'Then take it down.'

She just stood there, willing herself not to blindly obey him, as she once had.

His dark eyes glittered. 'If you don't, then I will.'

Jordan's hands lifted to pull out the pins which anchored her French pleat, her hair spilling down over her shoulders.

'Now come here,' he said, and moved his knees apart, drawing her gaze to those parts of his body which she'd been trying not to stare at.

Jordan stiffened. What did he want her to do?

'Put your right foot up here,' he said, patting a small area of the bed in front of him.

Relief loosened her frozen muscles, and she moved forward to do as he suggested.

He slipped off her shoe and tossed it aside, then peeled the short stocking down her leg, his fingers caressing her calf as he did so. Then her ankle, and then the sensitive sole of her foot.

'Mmm,' he said, once her leg was bare. 'Cream nail polish on your fingers, scarlet red on your toes. I wonder if your work colleagues know the real you, Jordan? The other foot, please.'

'And who is the real me?' she said, struggling

to keep her voice steady whilst he gave the other foot the same erotic treatment.

'You're a closet exhibitionist. And a sensualist.'

Jordan grimaced when he pulled her foot towards him, pressing her toes into him.

'Rub your foot up and down on me,' he said.

When she did, a raw groan broke from his lips.

'You see?' he said, grabbing her ankle and depositing her by then unsteady foot back on the floor.

She saw nothing, her mind having tipped from reality into that wildly erotic, heart-pounding world where desire ruled and pleasure beckoned.

'Come closer,' he commanded.

When she did, he dragged her panties down to her ankles, then bent forward to kiss her stomach.

Jordan's belly tightened under his lips, her hands lifting to rake through his hair. She groaned when he swirled his tongue in her navel, gasped when his hands slid between her legs, whimpered when his fingers slipped inside her…

His head suddenly lifted from her stomach. 'Don't let go yet,' he warned her, even whilst he continued the most intimate exploration of her body.

'Oh, God, Gino. I can't. I… Please… Please…'

'Now *you* are the impatient one. I like that. Would you like me inside you now? Tell me how much. Tell me,' he urged, his eyes like shining black coals as they gazed up at her.

'Stop tormenting me,' she cried.

'But I find I am enjoying it. It makes me feel good to see you this desperate for me.'

'Just do it, for pity's sake!'

She was on the bed and under him before she could utter another word. He hooked her ankles over his shoulders, then drove into her. Deep.

'Is this what you wanted?' he muttered as he pounded into her.

'Yes,' she panted. 'Yes.'

'You can come now,' he growled, just as she splintered apart in an orgasm which blew her mind even further than it was already.

Dimly, she heard him cry out, her senses no longer her own. She was lost, drowning in the heady sensation of his hot seed flooding her womb, exulting in the feel of his flesh pulsating in a rapturous tandem with her own.

It wasn't till some time afterwards, when their bodies had finally become as quiet as the room, that Jordan's brain kicked back into gear, her stomach somersaulting at the realisation that Gino hadn't used any protection.

Not that this was a total disaster. She was on the pill. But her own lack of thought in that regard—and, more to the point, *his*—was a real worry.

'Gino,' she said, her hands pushing at his shoulders.

'Yes, yes, I know. I'm heavy.'

'It's not that. I was just thinking…you…you didn't use a condom.'

He levered himself up onto his elbows and stared down at her.

'Are you saying I could have made you pregnant just now?'

'No. Pregnancy's not my concern. I'm on the pill.'

'I promise you I'm no risk to your health,' Gino reassured her. 'Look, are you hungry? I am.'

'I'm starving,' she confessed.

'The Room Service menu's over there, on that desk. In a leather folder. Check it out while I go run us both a bath.'

'Wait,' she said. 'I need to go to the loo first.'

'I'm not stopping you.'

'But I don't—' She broke off, thinking how she would have died rather than go to the bathroom in front of Chad. Yet when she'd lived with Gino they'd hidden nothing from each other.

But she wasn't living with Gino any more, came the timely reminder. She was living by herself. An independent, grown-up woman who liked her privacy.

'I'm sorry, Gino, but I'd prefer to use the bathroom alone.'

He stared at her in surprise, then shrugged. 'Whatever.'

Jordan hurried, feeling slightly silly at her stance. She'd just let him touch her in very private places, let him strip her and have sex with her. Let him see her come.

Now she had suddenly gone all shy and precious with him. It seemed they couldn't exactly take up where they'd left off after all. Ten years had gone by. She'd changed, even if he hadn't.

Gino was waiting outside the bathroom door, totally naked, whilst she'd drawn on one of the hotel's bathrobes.

'All yours,' she said, and bolted past him, not wanting to start staring again.

The Room Service menu was where he'd said it was.

And so was a plane ticket, lying next to it on the desk.

Jordan stared at it for a long moment.

Then she picked it up.

## CHAPTER FIVE

GINO found himself humming as he watched the tub fill, the bath gel having turned the water a pale green as well as providing some fragrant bubbles.

For the first time in years he felt light-hearted. And happy.

All because he'd found Jordan again.

It was as if the last ten years had been wiped away. He felt young again, and invincible. Jordan was still his woman—had been since the first day he'd set eyes on her.

She'd been working as a waitress back then, at an Italian restaurant not far from Sydney University, just across the road from the building site where Gino had been employed.

Although he'd been trying to opt out of everything Italian at that particular time in his life, the mouthwatering smell of his favourite pasta dishes had kept beckoning, and he'd finally given in to temptation and gone there for an evening meal.

Fate had sat him down at one of Jordan's tables.

The sexual chemistry between them had been instant and electric. He'd stayed on, eating more than he needed, just so he could keep talking to the beautiful blonde waitress who hadn't been able to take her eyes off him any more than he could her. He'd openly flirted with her, and she'd served him with a degree of attention which Gino had found both telling and seductive.

When she'd confided over his third cup of coffee that her flatmate had decided to drop out of university and go back home to live, leaving her to find the rent alone, Gino had grabbed the opportunity, saying he'd been looking for a place to live and asking would she consider having him as her flatmate?

His eyes must have told her that he wanted to be more than just her flatmate. So when she'd agreed to his moving in the next day, Gino had been a serious state of arousal even before he'd set foot in the place. He hadn't lasted more than half an hour before he had kissed her. One thing had quickly led to another, with Gino thanking his lucky stars that he'd come into that restaurant.

His discovering that Jordan was only nineteen—and a virgin—had been a huge shock. But subsequently a huge delight.

She'd become his perfect fantasy lover—her youth and inexperience allowing him to live out his own fantasy role as the masterful older male. He'd been thrilled by her falling for him despite thinking he was just a labourer, wallowing in her acceptance of him as a man in his own right. He'd revelled in the sexual power he'd held over her. What man wouldn't have? She was an incredibly beautiful girl, with a brilliant mind and a strength of character which was formidable.

Yet, in his arms, she was all sensual submission.

Not passive, though; Jordan was too passionate for passive.

He hadn't been able to keep his hands off her back then, quickly becoming addicted to the primal feelings she'd evoked in him. It seemed that hadn't changed. He could not wait to carry her into this bath and for their lovemaking to begin again.

A loud rapping on the bathroom door had Gino whirling round, his heart lurching with instant worry.

He snapped off the taps, then wrenched open the door. There she stood, the object of his desire, her lovely face coldly furious, her hands jammed into the pockets of the white towelling robe.

'I know I agreed that explanations could wait till the morning,' she snapped. 'But that was before I saw this.'

Gino's stomach rolled over when she pulled

her right hand from the robe pocket and held out his slightly crumpled plane ticket.

He'd forgotten that he'd left it on that damned desk, having emptied his suit pockets before changing clothes late this afternoon.

'This ticket is for tomorrow morning,' she swept on before he could say a word. 'Very early tomorrow morning. Which rather puts paid to your claim that you're up here for the weekend.'

'I wasn't going to take that flight, Jordan. Not after I ran into you. I was going to ring up and change it to Sunday.'

'You still lied to me, Gino.'

'I just twisted the truth a little.'

'Twisted the truth?' she repeated, with a caustic gleam in her eyes. 'And how would you describe giving someone a false name? Because this ticket is made out to a Mr Gino Bortelli.'

'Jordan, I—'

'I take it that's your real name?' she interrupted savagely. 'Bortelli? Not Salieri, like you told me ten years ago?'

Gino tried to keep calm, but a very true panic hovered in the wings of his mind. 'Salieri is my mother's maiden name. I took it temporarily when I came to Sydney for reasons of privacy.'

'Reasons of privacy?' she repeated scathingly. 'Like, people might recognise you as what, exactly? A rock star in hiding?'

'No, as Gino Bortelli.'

'Sorry, Gino. But I'm none the wiser.'

'My family are rather big in the construction business. I didn't want any special favours when I first came to Sydney. I'd not long finished an engineering degree at university in Rome, and I—'

'Excuse me?' she snapped. 'Are you telling me you're a qualified *engineer?* I thought you were a labourer.'

'That's what I was working as when I first met you.'

Jordan looked totally bewildered. 'But *why?* That would be like me still working as a waitress instead of a lawyer.'

Gino sighed, then reached for the other bathrobe hanging on the back of the door. There seemed little point in staying naked. The erotic night he'd been planning was well and truly over.

'Could we go out into the other room?' he suggested, after he drew the robe on and tied the sash around his waist. 'I could do with a drink.'

He strode past her out into the hotel room proper, heading for the mini-bar.

'Do you want a glass of wine?' he asked, glancing over his shoulder at Jordan as she reluctantly followed him. 'There's a half-bottle of red here which isn't too bad.'

'No, thanks,' she returned crisply. 'What I want to know is why you lied to me about so many things.'

'Perhaps you should sit down?' he suggested, indicating the sofa opposite the television.

She didn't sit down, moving past the sofa to stand in front of the window, with her arms crossed and her eyes still sceptical.

Gino poured himself a full glass of wine, taking a decent swallow before turning to face her across the room.

'I was tired after studying for years. Tired of being pushed by my parents to be an over-achiever. It's a common enough phenomenon in Italian families. I demanded a year off, to just be myself and not my father's only son. I wanted to earn my own money. Be totally independent. Live a simpler, less stressful life. That was why I decided to work with my hands, and why I changed my name. Because I didn't want my employer recognising the Bortelli name and treating me differently.'

Jordan frowned. 'People would recognise the Bortelli name even out here in Australia?'

This was the moment Gino had been dreading. But the truth had to come out—especially if he wanted to continue seeing Jordan. And he did, very much.

'I think you might have misunderstood something about me all those years ago,' he began carefully. 'I didn't exactly come to Sydney straight from Rome. After I finished my degree I went home to my family first.'

'So where in Italy does your family live?'

'My family doesn't live in Italy, Jordan. They migrated to Melbourne not long after I was born. That's where they live. Melbourne.'

She stared at him with stunned blue eyes. 'You're saying you're Australian?'

'I hold dual citizenship. Both Italian and Australian.'

'Why didn't you tell me any of this ten years ago?'

'I wish now that I had. But back then I was also tired of being Italian. I needed a change. I needed to find myself. Then, after I met you, Jordan, I just needed you.'

She stared at him, her eyes going cold again. 'Only till your *family* needed you, Gino. Then you dropped me like a hot cake.'

Gino sighed. She didn't understand. She

could never understand what it was like to be the only son in an Italian household.

'If anything happens to me, Gino,' his father used to say all the time, 'then it is your job to look after the family. Your mother and your sisters. And the business, of course.'

'And what about this weekend, Gino?' Jordan threw at him. 'Was it to be more of the same? You needed a change so you came to Sydney? Because Sydney is full of silly girls only too willing to give you sex?'

'I came to Sydney on business,' Gino pointed out, his sense of honour totally offended by her accusations. 'I was going to fly back to Melbourne tomorrow, remember?'

'Sorry,' she quipped sarcastically. 'I momentarily forgot under the pressure of all these amazing revelations. So you ran into me, and you thought, Wow, there's good old Jordan— the dumb bird who let me screw her every which way. I'll bet she's good for another go. I'll just give her a line of bull. She'd believe anything I tell her. And presto—you were right. I fell for it, hook, line and sinker.'

'Jordan, stop it!' Gino said, appalled at the way things were going.

'Stop what?' she snapped, her blue eyes blazing at him. 'Stop telling you how it really is? Don't the ladies do that to you down in Melbourne? No, of course they don't. You're a bigshot down there. They probably crawl to you on their hands and knees. Do you have a girlfriend, Gino? Do you make her go without panties? Do you do it to her all the time, the way you used to do it to me?'

Gino felt his own temper begin to rise. He'd tried to be patient with her. Tried to explain. But she seemed determined to twist everything in her mind, to make everything they'd once shared sound ugly and sordid.

'What in hell's wrong with you?' he snarled. 'Why are you trying to spoil everything? Look, I'm sorry I didn't tell you the truth back then. But I did have my reasons. And I'm sorry I left you the way I did. But I had my reasons for that as well. My father was dying, damn it. I *had* to go home.'

'Then why didn't you come back? After your father died? Tell me that. You obviously had the resources to. Yet you chose not to. What kind of love was that, Gino?'

'You really want to know?'

'Yes. I really want to know.'

Gino could see that all was lost. So what did it matter if he told her that last unpalatable truth?

'I didn't come back because you weren't Italian.'

Her mouth fell open. But no words came out.

'I promised my father on his deathbed that when I married I would marry an Italian girl.'

'You have to be kidding,' she blurted out.

'Unfortunately, no.' He knew only too well that he had been afraid that if he came back to Jordan he would forget his promise and marry her.

She shook her head at him, her eyes dropping

limply to her sides. 'And have you?' she asked in a dull, flat voice. 'Married an Italian girl?'

'You think I would lie about something like that?'

'I have no idea what you would lie about, Gino. I don't know you. I never did. The man I lived with—and fell in love with—wasn't real. He was a pretend man. A fantasy lover. The real Gino is a stranger to me. So I'm asking you again. Are you married?'

'I told you. I'm not married.'

'But you do have a girlfriend, don't you?'

'Yes,' he bit out. 'I do.'

'So you're a cheat as well as a liar!'

Gino sucked in sharply. No one had spoken to him like this in his whole life.

His shock deepened when she suddenly unsashed her robe and pushed it back off her shoulders, letting it drop to the floor. For a long moment she stood there, totally naked, her chin tipped up as she watched him devour every beautiful inch of her.

When his flesh automatically responded, Gino's fingers tightened defensively around his wine glass. He didn't know what she was up to, but he suspected that if he made any move to touch her she would scream the place down.

'You like what you see, Gino?' she said at last, in a challenging fashion.

Gino's teeth clenched down hard in his jaw. The Jordan he'd known ten years ago had never been a bitch. The Jordan standing before him now was doing a very good imitation of one.

Perversely, it made him want her all the more.

'Take a good long look, because you're never going to see me like this again. Not that you'd overly care,' she went on savagely, as she moved over to snatch up her clothes. 'You'll fly home to your girlfriend and you won't give this little interlude a second thought. You won't even feel guilty.'

She couldn't have been more wrong. He'd never be able to put tonight—or her—out of his mind. And guilt was going to be his constant companion from now on.

As for Claudia… Gino could see that he would have to break off their relationship. She was a very nice girl, but she wanted to get married.

After this, marriage was permanently off Gino's agenda. If he couldn't marry Jordan, then he wouldn't marry anyone.

In an amazingly short period of time Jordan was fully dressed, looking exactly as she had when he'd first seen her tonight. Except for her hair. As she hooked her bag over her shoulder she tossed her head at him, flicking her hair back from her face.

'I never forgot you, you know,' she threw at him. 'Never. A girlfriend of mine said it was because you were unfinished business. She said it was a pity I couldn't look you up, so that I could see you weren't as fantastic as I thought you were. And she was right. You're not. Oh, you're still great at sex—I'll give you that. You know exactly how to turn a girl on.

But that's a small talent in the wider scheme of things. I want a man who knows what he wants and goes after it. Who doesn't let *anything* stand in his way. You're obviously not that kind of man.'

'How do you know?'

'I know,' she said, with a curl of her top lip. 'Actions speak a lot louder than words, Gino.'

'You're making a big mistake,' he said as she headed for the door.

She reached for the doorknob, then stopped to cast a cold glance over her shoulder. 'No, I'm *ending* a big mistake. You're finished business now,' she said, then wrenched open the door. *'Ciao.'*

# CHAPTER SIX

JORDAN managed to make it home without shedding a tear. Pride prevented her from breaking down in the hotel, or during the taxi ride home. But the moment she was alone, with her door safely locked behind her, everything came crashing in around her.

Her legs suddenly buckled and she sank to the floor where she stood. Her knees hit the tiled foyer first, and her cry was not one of physical pain but of emotional distress.

'Oh, Gino,' she sobbed as her head tipped forward into her hands.

And there she stayed, as if she was in prayer.

But she wasn't praying, she was weeping. And despairing.

For there were no illusions left for her now.

All these years she'd thought that her memory of Gino had been spoiling her relationships with men. And maybe that was true. But it had been a bittersweet memory, because she'd always believed Gino had loved her.

But he hadn't loved her. He'd merely wanted her, the way he'd wanted her tonight. Not for anything lasting, just for sex.

That discovery had been bad enough. Finding out that his whole persona had been an illusion was even worse. He wasn't some struggling Italian immigrant, trying to make a good life for himself through hard work. He was a silver-tail, slumming it for a while up here in Sydney. Roughing it—with her.

Tonight had just been a shorter version of what he'd done ten years ago.

Okay, so he probably *had* been going to change his flight till Sunday. But his motive had still been totally selfish. After all, why look a gift-horse in the mouth?

And, brother, what a gift-horse she was

where he was concerned. Fifteen miserable minutes and she'd been up there in his room, ready and willing to take her clothes off. Ready for just about anything.

If she hadn't found that plane ticket he would have had his wicked way with her for the whole weekend, then flown off back to Melbourne, to his real life and his real girlfriend.

Thinking about that had Jordan sitting back on her heels and wiping the tears from the cheeks. What on earth was she doing, crying over such a man? He was a bastard through and through.

Scooping in a gathering breath, Jordan got to her feet and walked quickly to her bedroom. No more was she going to let Gino Betolli spoil things for her. No more. When Chad rang her in the morning she would accept his proposal of marriage, and she would do her level best not to think of Gino ever again.

But such resolves were easy to make,

Jordan came to realise, once she'd stripped off and stepped into the shower. Living them was not so easy.

Her body—especially her naked body—kept reminding her of Gino, the after-effects of his torrid lovemaking conspiring to keep him in her mind. Just moving the soapy sponge lightly between her legs made her belly tighten and her breath catch.

This was what had happened to her when she'd lived with Gino. She'd been in a perpetual state of arousal. Her flesh had craved his constantly, craved release from the sexual tension he created in her.

It craved release now…

Jordan dropped the sponge, then slowly slid her back down the wet tiles till she was sitting on the shower floor. Her arms lifted to wrap around her drawn-up knees, her head dropping forward as she surrendered once more to tears.

'Oh, Gino,' she cried. 'Gino…'

* * *

The phone woke her, its persistent ringing getting through the blissful oblivion which had finally descended on Jordan last night, courtesy of the painkillers she'd taken—strong ones she used when she had a migraine. Unfortunately, they had to tendency to leave her a little groggy the next day.

Rolling over with a groan, she picked up the extension near her bed and shoved it between her ear and the pillow.

'Yes?' Not exactly a breezy hello.

'Jordan? Is that you?'

The sound of Chad's voice had her sitting up and pushing her tangled hair out of her eyes. A glance at the bedside clock shocked her. It was nearly ten.

'Yes, it's me,' she said more brightly. 'Have you arrived yet?'

'Just. Thought I'd ring you before I got out in the New York traffic. You sounded sleepy just now. Did I wake you?'

'Sort of. I…um… I had a late night.'

'A late night doing what?'

A rush of guilt had Jordan being grateful Chad couldn't see her. Not that he was all that intuitive. Chad was the sort of man who only saw what he wanted to see. He honestly thought her turning down his proposal was just her playing hard to get. He clearly had no doubts that she would say yes, even leaving the engagement ring with her—a family heirloom which had belonged to his grandmother.

'Working,' she lied. 'I have to wrap up the Johnson case on Monday, remember?'

'You've become a bit obsessed by that case, don't you think?'

'No.' Her client was a young woman whose husband had been killed in a train derailment. Shock and grief had sent her into early labour, with their premature baby boy not making it. When the government had finally offered her compensation, several years later, they hadn't included anything for the pain and loss of her child. They'd called her son a foetus, not worthy of consideration as a human being. She'd come to Jordan wanting not a fortune, but justice.

Jordan aimed to get justice for her. Which she would—if she could get her head into gear and prepare a killer of a closing argument this weekend.

'You work too hard, Jordan.'

'I enjoy my work, Chad.' More than enjoyed. She'd feel totally empty without it.

'Have you thought about what I asked you the other night?'

Jordan's chest tightened. She'd known he'd get round to this sooner or later.

'Yes,' she said.

'And?'

This was it: the moment of truth. Did she have the courage of her convictions? Or was she going to weaken and let Gino keep spoiling things for her?

She had a choice. She could pine over a relationship which had been doomed from the start. Or she could choose a new relationship which had everything going for it.

Okay, not quite everything. But everything that mattered. Great sex was not the be all and end all, she reasoned. Besides, it wasn't that Chad was a hopeless lover. He certainly wasn't. The problem—if there was one—lay in her own responses. Gino had somehow programmed her not to respond totally to any other man. He, and he alone, could make her lose her head and lose control. Last night had proved that.

But this phenomenon only occurred when he was around. He wasn't around now. He would never be around again.

The time had come to stop hiding behind her illogical passion for a man who, by his own admission, would never marry her. Next year she would be thirty. In ten years she'd be forty.

Time to make a decision.

'Yes, Chad,' she said firmly. 'I will marry you.'

## CHAPTER SEVEN

GINO was on the top floor of his latest sky-scraper construction-in-progress, making his way carefully along a not-too-wide girder, when his cellphone rang. He waited till he reached the relative safety of a corner before fishing it out of his pocket.

'Gino Bortelli,' he said, one arm wrapped securely around a post. The breeze was quite strong up that high.

'What is this I hear about you breaking up with Claudia?' came his mother's highly accented voice.

Gino smothered a sigh. The grapevine in the Italian community was very fast and usually accurate.

'It's no big deal, Mum. She wasn't right for

me, and I wasn't right for her. We agreed to go our separate ways.'

'That is not the way I hear it, Gino. Claudia is very upset with you.'

Very upset that she wasn't marrying into the Bortelli money would be more like it.

Gino had been astounded at how vicious Claudia had become when he'd told her it was over between them. Suddenly she'd shown her true colours, using quite obscene language which everyone in the restaurant had heard. There'd been no hint of a broken heart, just ambition thwarted. After she'd flounced out all the other patrons in the place had stared at him, making Gino wish he'd chosen to break up with her in a more discreet and private place.

That had been last Sunday—two days ago. In hindsight, he was surprised it had taken his mother this long to find out. Maybe he should have told her himself. But since returning to Melbourne on Saturday he hadn't wanted to have anything to do with his family.

It was because of them that he'd had to leave Jordan in the first place. And he'd not been able to go back for her. They'd sucked him emotionally dry till he no longer wanted get married and have children. The last ten years had been filled with nothing but unending responsibility and pressure, with him putting his mother's and sisters' needs first, never his own.

But enough was enough.

'Claudia was more in love with my money than she was with me, Mum,' he said firmly. 'Trust me on that. Look, I can't stay and chat. I'm working.'

His mother sighed. 'You work too hard, Gino. You should take some time off.'

'Maybe I will. But not today.'

'Before you go, did you decide what you were going to do with that derelict site in Sydney? The one Papa bought all those years ago?'

'Everything's underway. It's going to be a twenty-storey tower with apartments on the top ten floors, office space on the lower ten, shops on the ground floor, and parking underneath. I signed the contract with the architect last Friday.'

'That is good, Gino. Papa would be pleased.'

'How can he be pleased about anything, Mum, when he's dead?'

'Gino! How can you say such a wicked thing? Have you no faith? Your papa is watching over us from heaven. He would be very proud of you.'

Gino shook his head. There was no arguing with his mother's faith. So he didn't bother.

'He would be even prouder,' she added, 'if you married and carried on the Bortelli name.'

'I am still only thirty-six, Mum. I have plenty of time for that yet. Look, I have to go.'

'Will you be coming to dinner next Sunday?'

His mother held a big family get-together on the last Sunday of every month. Gino usually attended. He liked playing with his nieces and nephews. But he hated the thought of being bombarded by questions over why Claudia wasn't with him.

'I can't, Mum. Sorry. I have to go to Sydney to meet up with this architect. He wants to show me some preliminary plans.'

Not true. But his mother wasn't to know that. Still, he would have to go somewhere. Maybe to the snow? He liked skiing, and there was still some good snow in the ski-fields. He'd tire himself out every day and make sure he fell asleep each night the moment his head hit the pillow.

He hadn't slept well since returning from Sydney, his mind constantly tormented with what ifs.

What if he hadn't made that foolish promise to his father?

What if he'd been able to go back for Jordan without feeling lousy?

What if he'd told her the truth about himself *before* they'd gone up to his hotel room last Friday night?

This last *what if* was easily answered: he'd been too aroused to delay, or to risk Jordan rejecting him after his explanations.

His need for her had transcended commonsense.

Was he still in love with her? he wondered. Or did he just want to escape with her again, as he had all those years ago?

She'd claimed she'd never forgotten him.

Gino believed her.

How could either of them forget the fantasy life they'd lived together, such an erotically charged existence, full of passion and pleasure? But underneath all the sex had been true affection. He hadn't just used Jordan, he'd truly cared for her—and she for him.

But they were different people now. She was more cynical and less trusting. And he was…well, he was trapped by his previous deceptions.

And yet he would give anything, *do* anything, to be with her like that again.

'You should spend more time with your family, Gino,' his mother chided.

Gino's teeth clenched down hard in his jaw, the cords in his neck standing out.

'I have to go, Mum. *Ciao.*'

He grimaced as he hung up, the Italian word for goodbye reminding him of the last time he'd heard it. On Jordan's lips, as she swept out of the hotel room. And out of his life.

His life…

Gino glanced down at the city spread out below him. He was on top of the world so to speak. On top of the world financially as well as professionally. He had more money than he would ever need, a fancy penthouse and a fancy car: a Ferrari, no less.

As for Bortelli Constructions… Although it had already been a well-known building company when he'd taken it over, under his guiding hand the company had gone from strength to strength, gaining an enviable reputation for reliability and quality. His hard work and astute business decisions had made every member of the Bortelli family millionaires several times over, and he himself was close to becoming a billionaire.

But such successes counted for nothing if you weren't happy.

Jordan's various accusations and taunts still haunted him.

Perhaps because they were true. Technically, he had lied and cheated. But he wasn't the coward she thought he was.

He *did* know what he wanted.

Her.

But what was the point in pursuing her when she would not welcome his attentions?

Gino could see no way of her getting Jordan to spend time with him—short of kidnapping her and imprisoning her in some secluded place with him.

That idea had some appeal as a male fantasy.

Unfortunately, he couldn't see the adult Jordan being one of those female hostages who would ever feel kindly towards her captor. When she'd stood naked in front of him and told him he'd never see her like that again he'd believed her.

Gino sighed, then headed for the steel cage which would carry him down to the ground again. It was knock-off time in the building trade. Not so for the boss, however, who had to go back to his office in the city and make sure the administrative wheels of Bortelli Constructions were kept turning.

Half an hour later his hard hat had been discarded and he was sitting behind his desk, a strong mug of coffee on his right and a load of correspondence in front of him. The clock on the wall was just ticking over to five when he picked up an envelope marked 'Personal', which his secretary hadn't opened.

Gino winced at the thought that it might be hate-mail from Claudia.

No, he decided as he ripped open the envelope. She wouldn't write. She'd e-mail or text message him. Girls like Claudia never put pen to paper these days.

Gino found himself staring down at a gold-embossed sheet of paper.

It was an invitation from Stedley & Parkinson.

Mr Frank Jones, the senior partner of the Sydney branch, was inviting Mr Gino Bortelli—and partner—to a new client dinner on the following Saturday evening in their boardroom. The arrival time was seven-thirty, the dress black tie. His RSVP was required by Friday; an e-mail address was provided for his reply.

Gino stared at the invitation for a good twenty seconds without drawing a breath. Then he gulped in some much needed air before letting it out with a long, slow sigh.

Fate, it seemed, had stepped in to give him one last chance with Jordan.

For surely the star of Stedley & Parkinson's litigation section would have recently gained a new client or two? If so, she would probably be obliged to attend this dinner.

Gino's heart raced with the thought of seeing Jordan again—especially in a situation where she could not think he was deliberately stalking her. Their running into each other again would appear to be sheer coincidence. Which, in a way, it would be.

He wouldn't be taking a partner, of course. He no longer had a partner. Not that he would have taken Claudia anywhere near Jordan.

Gino wondered if Adrian had received an invitation.

No, probably not. Adrian had told him he'd used Stedley and Parkinson's for legal work before. Which meant he wouldn't be a new client.

Still, it was likely that he'd been to such a dinner before, giving him first-hand knowledge of what kind of a do this was, and especially who attended from Stedley & Parkinson.

Reaching for his cellphone, Gino looked up the menu of numbers he kept in there, located Adrian's number and punched it in.

'Adrian Palmer,' Adrian answered straight away.

Although one of Australia's most up-and-coming young architects, Adrian didn't use a secretary, or a proper office. He worked out of his high-rise apartment, situated in the middle of Sydney's CBD.

'Hi, Adrian. Gino Bortelli here.'

'Gino! I was just working on the plans for your building. I think you're going to be seriously pleased.'

'That's great, Adrian. Look, I've received an invitation in the mail from Stedley & Parkinson.'

'For one of their new client dinners, I presume?'

'Yes. Have you ever been to one?'

'Yep—last month, actually. They have these dinners once a month. You should go, Gino. The food's always great, and so is the wine. Of course that means you'll have to fly up. But it's tax-deductible.'

'It says black tie. That's a bit formal for a dinner in a boardroom, isn't it?'

'That would have come down from Mr Stedley, the American owner. He's Ivy League and one of the country-club brigade over there in the States. He's a strong believer in social networking. Encourages his employees to socialise together, too.'

'You sound like you've met this guy. Don't tell me he flies over from the States to attend?'

'Nope. Met his son, though. Chad Stedley. He's doing a stint out here in the Sydney office. They sat me next to him at this dinner. Quite a talker. Got the story of his life between courses. Had a gorgeous-looking girlfriend. Another of their lawyers—Jordan something-or-other.'

Gino's heart screeched to a halt even whilst his head whirled. Jordan had said there was no special man in her life. Yet a month ago she'd been this Chad Stedley's girlfriend?

There seemed only two solutions to this conundrum. She'd either broken up with Stedley since then. A possibility, given the difficult nature of relationships these days. Or she'd lied last Friday night. Which didn't seem possible. Jordan had a real thing about lying.

'Jordan Gray?' Gino said.

'Yep. That was her name. You know her, do you?'

'I used to.'

'No kidding? An old girlfriend?'

'Something like that.'

'It's a small world, isn't it?'

'It seems so.'

'In that case you should think twice before bringing your current girlfriend along. You know what women are like. And that Jordan's a real looker.'

'Haven't got a current girlfriend,' Gino admitted. 'I was thinking of going alone.'

'I see. Well, I wouldn't count on your getting together again with this Jordan, if I were you,' Adrian advised drily. 'I gathered from the

Stedley son and heir that an engagement was just around the corner.'

'An engagement!' Gino exclaimed, before he could think better of it.

'Yep. If that thought upsets you, then perhaps you shouldn't go at all.'

*Upset* him?

Already a tidal wave of fury was building up on his horizon. If Jordan had lied to him…

A boyfriend was bad enough. But if she'd willingly had sex with him, then gone home to her fiancé, he wasn't sure how he'd handle it.

'No, no,' Gino said with pretend nonchalance. 'No sweat. It's been years since Jordan and I were an item. But I wouldn't mind seeing her again, having a chat about old times.'

Plus a chat about very recent times, Gino vowed darkly. Namely last Friday night.

'In that case be discreet. Chad Stedley came across as the controlling type. He might not like his girl's ex showing up in her life again.'

'He sounds delightful.'

'He's super-rich.'

'Meaning?'

'Women will put up with a lot to marry a super-rich guy.'

'Is that the voice of experience talking?'

'Hell, no. I'm rich, but not super-rich. Yet. Still, you must have come across a few gold-digging types. The Bortellis were listed as one the richest one hundred Australian families last year.'

'Ahh,' Gino said. 'You looked us up?'

'I always like to know who I'm doing business with, Gino. I steer well clear of the entrepreneurial type who has to borrow squillions, or relies on selling off the plan for his cashflow.'

'Very sensible.'

'If you do come to Sydney you could drop by and have a look at my preliminary plans.'

'I haven't decided whether I'll come yet. I might go to the snow instead.'

'That might be a wiser course of action.'

'Yes,' Gino said slowly 'It might.'

But Gino wasn't feeling wise.

If Jordan *had* lied to him…

There was only one way to find out in advance of Saturday night. He would put Confidential Investigations back on the job. That gave them three and a half days to find out if Jordan had broken up with this Chad Stedley or not.

More than enough time, he would imagine. He would also see if they could find out if Jordan would be attending this dinner.

At the same time he would send an e-mail to the RSVP address, accepting Mr Frank Jones's invitation to the dinner.

# CHAPTER EIGHT

JORDAN reluctantly went through the motions of getting ready: same little black dress as last time, same shoes and jewellery.

Her hair she didn't have to do, thank goodness. She'd been to the hairdressers that morning, and had it shampooed and gently blowdried, giving her slightly wayward waves some control, but not straightening them too much. Her make-up took her less than ten minutes: just foundation, a touch of blusher, lipgloss and two coats of mascara.

Jordan rarely wore much make-up. Never had.

By half-past six she was ready—or as ready as she was ever going to be. Her taxi had been booked for seven, which left thirty minutes to do what? Watch half of an hour-long television show? Or have a glass of white wine and try to relax?

The second option won, hands down.

There was an already opened bottle of reisling in the door of her fridge—a fruity, slightly sweet wine, which Chad would have despised, but which Jordan liked. She poured herself a small glass and carried it through her living room, heading for her front balcony.

Jordan slid back the glass door, giving a small shiver as she stepped into the cool evening air. Fortunately it wasn't too windy, the sea breeze quite gentle. Darkness had fallen some time back, the lights giving a magical quality to Sydney's two most famous icons, which were both visible from her seventh-floor apartment. The bridge on her right looked like a huge jewelled coat-hanger, whilst across the harbour the sailed roof of the Opera House resembled the set from a sci-fi movie.

Jordan sighed as she leant against the railing

and sipped her wine, her mind swiftly distracted from the lovely view to the evening ahead.

She didn't want to go to this month's new client dinner.

But she simply couldn't get out of it. Not unless she had a very good reason.

When she'd told Chad during his early-morning call that she didn't want to go, not without him, he'd been flattered but insistent.

'You've taken on a new client this month, haven't you?'

'Yes,' she'd admitted. An angry young man who wanted to sue his employer for unfair dismissal after the boss had discovered he was a homosexual.

'Then you have to go, darling. Rules are rules. Just make sure you wear your engagement ring. Let all the men there know you're taken.'

Jordan had come away from that phone call just a tad unsure of her decision to marry Chad.

During his calls this week he'd become quite bossy with her. And demanding. He really seemed to think she was going to give up working once they were married and living in the States.

As if she would!

She'd also been quite put out when he'd been less than effusive in his congratulations over her winning all that compensation money for Sharni Johnson. He hadn't sounded as if he cared about her success at all!

Yet she was expected to rave over how his 'wonderful' friends had thrown him all those welcome home parties. So far he'd gone out somewhere different every night.

Somehow Jordan doubted he'd told any of the females attending these dos that *he* was taken. Chad liked being the centre of attention.

Jordan wasn't jealous, but she resented double standards.

Guilt consumed her with this last thought. After all, she hadn't exactly been Little Miss Innocent since Chad had gone away, had she?

Over a week had gone by since she'd gone

to Gino's hotel room, but the memory of her behaviour still haunted her.

She'd been putty in Gino's hands, quickly reverting to the naïve little fool she'd been ten years ago.

He'd said, 'Come with me'—and she had. He'd said, 'Don't come'—and she hadn't.

That was Gino's *modus operandi*. He commanded and she obeyed—and how she'd loved it!

Fortunately, fate had come to her rescue in the form of that plane ticket before she'd behaved even more foolishly.

Some damage had already been done, however. The damage which came when a woman experienced that level of sexual excitement, and the ecstasy which inevitably followed. Difficult to go back to the mundane after that. Difficult to forget.

That had always been her problem where Gino was concerned.

Forgetting…

Let's face it, Jordan, the voice of cold, hard reality piped up. You're never going to forget that man. You can marry Chad and go live in the States, put thousand of miles between you. But Gino's always going to be there, in your head.

Jordan groaned, tipped up her glass and swallowed the rest of her wine with one gulp. Then she whirled and headed back inside, to collect her evening bag and her keys.

At the last moment she remembered what Chad had asked her to do: wear the engage-ment ring which he'd left with her but which she hadn't as yet put on—even though she'd now accepted his proposal.

Did that omission say something?

It was not a ring she would have chosen, Jordan thought, as she hurried into the bedroom and retrieved it from a drawer. It was too fussy: a huge ruby, surrounded by two rows of diamonds, and on top of that the setting was yellow gold.

Jordan liked white gold. Or silver.

And she liked simplicity.

Of course Chad hadn't actually chosen this ring, she conceded. It was a family heirloom, having once belonged to his grandmother, who'd willed it to him when she died, to be given to his bride.

Jordan had been touched by the sentiment. But she suddenly wondered, as she slipped the ring on, if she'd be able to cope with Chad's high-powered and tradition-filled family—not to mention all his 'wonderful' friends. They sounded just a little overpowering.

It was one thing to live with him here, in Australia. Things were very easy-going here. But what would life be like in America? She'd never travelled there, her one and only overseas trip being to Europe, with most of her time spent in Italy.

No omission there. She'd stupidly thought she might find Gino. But she hadn't, of course. How could she have when she'd been looking for the wrong name?

Jordan gritted her teeth. Gino again.

Thinking of Gino reaffirmed her decision to marry Chad.

Okay, so Chad wasn't perfect. He was a touch arrogant. And obviously quite spoiled by his very wealthy, very indulgent parents.

No way was he as hard-working as she was.

But he wasn't a conniving, conning, cheating bastard.

*And* he wanted to marry her.

Whereas Gino…

'Enough of Gino,' she muttered under her breath as she swept out of her apartment. 'I'm going to marry Chad and that's that!'

# CHAPTER NINE

KERRY usually looked forward to the new client dinners. But tonight she would much rather have been out with Ben.

Running into him last Friday night—and finding out he was still single—had been a very pleasant surprise. He was her one ex that she truly regretted having broken up with. They hadn't argued or anything. Ben had simply had the urge to travel.

Now he was back in Australia, and obviously wanted to take up with her where they'd left off. They'd spent most of the weekend together, and a few evenings this week, with Ben eager to take her to a concert tonight.

But, as Frank's PA, Kerry was obliged not

only to attend this dinner, but to help hostess the event. Frank was a widower, with no new partner, and he had no idea how to organise anything. It was always left to her to do the place settings, hire a caterer, buy the wine, choose the menu, and then make sure every-thing went off without a hiccup.

This month she'd chosen a new caterer, who was expensive but who came highly recom-mended. They'd also provided everything, right down to fresh flowers for the table. The chef was top drawer, having worked in several five-star hotels. The waiters were also experi-enced professionals, not fly-by-night casuals like some catering firms used.

Kerry still thought it would have been less trouble to go to a restaurant. But Stedley & Parkinson preferred the intimacy and the privacy of their boardroom.

Admittedly the boardroom was well equipped for such a function, having an excel-lent kitchen attached, plus two powder rooms just outside in the hallway. The boardroom itself was a very spacious and impressive room, with a huge mahogany table which comfortably seated twenty-four. The floors were polished wood and the walls white, a perfect backdrop for the colourful Australian artwork which decorated them. All originals, they were landscapes from famous artists such as Pro Hart and Albert Namatjira.

Kerry could understand why Frank chose to host these dinners here. She just resented the added workload, which was why she'd found this new catering firm, leaving her little to do except work out who would sit where.

Of course that wasn't always as easy as it looked. Certain tensions among the staff at Stedley & Parkinson had to be addressed, with rival lawyers kept well apart. And there was always a surfeit of men, too, even amongst the new clients. Kerry was relieved that Jordan was coming. She'd put her between Mr Bortelli—who wasn't bringing a partner—and

Mr McKee, Jordan's client, who also wasn't bringing a partner.

All up, eighteen people would be at the dinner: six lawyers, their six most important new clients—four of whom had brought partners—and Frank and herself.

Of course not every new client the practice took on was invited. Only the ones who had serious money, or whose cases might provide the most publicity. Jordan's new clients were always invited, because she took on cases which the press—and the public—found interesting.

As Kerry walked around the boardroom, making sure all the place-names were right, she wondered if Jordan would wear something different this month. Last month she'd turned up in the same outfit she'd worn the month before—a classic, but boring little black dress, with a high scooped neckline, long sleeves and a straight, not-too-tight skirt which covered up far too much of her excellent legs. The double-strand pearl necklace she always wore with it was just as prim and proper, though her shoes were not too bad: black, strappy and high.

Nevertheless, now that Jordan was engaged to Prince Charming she would definitely have to upgrade her wardrobe from off-the-peg-working-girl clothes to designer gear.

Men like Chad Stedley expected their wives to outshine everyone else. Jordan might not realise it yet, but she was about to enter a totally new world, where fashion and appearances would be critical to her success as Mrs Chad Stedley.

No longer could she get away with dressing the way she did. Some serious shopping was called for before Chad came back from the States. And Kerry was just the girl to go with her and give her advice.

'Oh, doesn't everything look lovely!'

Kerry glanced up with a smile already forming on her face.

'Speak of the devil,' she said, on seeing Jordan. 'I like your hair.' Too bad about the dress, Kerry thought ruefully.

'Everyone's still up in Frank's office, having pre-dinner drinks,' Jordan said.

'Yes—so why aren't you?'

'I walked by the door and simply couldn't bear to go in and make meaningless chit-chat. So I dropped my purse off in my office and came straight down here to talk to you.'

Kerry grinned. 'Coward. You just don't want to— Oh, my God! You're wearing the engagement ring. Here, give me a good look at it. Oh, my, it's fabulous! Chad must have picked it out. I know you, Jordan. You would have chosen a single diamond solitaire, half that size, set in a simple claw setting.'

Jordan shook her head wryly at her friend. 'And you'd be right. This is actually a family heirloom.'

'How did he get it to you? By international courier?'

'No. He left it with me before he went overseas.'

'Because he knew you'd eventually say yes.'

'How could he have known?'

Kerry rolled her eyes at her friend. 'Because multimillionaires like him don't get turned down.'

'I'm not marrying him for his money, Kerry.'

'I know that. You're marrying him because you love him, and because you've finally got over that Italian fellow. Speaking of Italians— I hope you don't have anything against Italian men in general, because I've seated you next to one tonight.'

'Oh?'

'He's Henry's new client. Contracts and mergers. I didn't expect him to accept the invitation, since he lives in Melbourne. But, lo and behold, he did.'

Jordan's heart skipped a beat. It couldn't possibly be Gino, could it? Would fate be that cruel?

'I hear he's quite a hunk,' Kerry added. 'And filthy rich. He's a builder. Of seriously big buildings.'

Jordan's chest tightened. Oh, no, she thought with a mixture of disbelief and despair. It had to be Gino.

Fortunately, Kerry was in the process of checking the name cards and wasn't looking at her. Jordan didn't want her friend putting two and two together. And she just might if she saw the near panic which was bubbling up inside Jordan.

'Does he have a name, this Italian?' she asked, using her extra-cool court voice—the one she could conjure up no matter how she felt inside.

'What? Oh—Bortelli. Gino Bortelli. Look, I'll have to love you and leave you, Jordan. I can hear voices coming down the hallway. I need to let the caterer know that everyone's arriving.'

She bustled off without giving Jordan a second glance, which was just as well.

For the life of her Jordan didn't know how she hadn't fainted. All the blood had definitely drained from her face when she'd heard that dreaded name, her head swirling alarmingly.

She stumbled over and gripped the back of the nearest chair, afraid to turn around and face the main doorway. The voices were much closer, indicating that people were moving into the room.

'Ahh…so there you are, Jordan,' a male voice boomed.

Jordan winced. It was Frank—Kerry's boss. And *her* boss.

Impossible to do anything but turn round. Yet she knew as she did so that Frank wouldn't be alone. He would have their most valuable new client with him: the very wealthy Mr Gino Bortelli.

Despite being mentally prepared for the encounter, Jordan was still stunned by the sight of Gino, dressed to kill in a magnificent black dinner suit, complete with a white dress-shirt and a black bow-tie. Stunned, too, by what she saw in his black eyes.

Not surprise, as she would have imagined if this was a cruel twist of fate. But coldness. And contempt.

The realisation that he'd known she would be here tonight was instantaneous. The only question remaining was how come? Jordan hadn't told him where she worked.

Gino should have been as shocked as she was. But he wasn't. Not at all.

Which meant what?

Somehow she managed a polite smile, but all the while her head was spinning with unanswered questions.

'Hello, Frank,' she said, reefing her eyes away from the man by his side.

'Mr McKee was looking for you,' Frank said, a touch irritably.

'Really? Where is he?'

'He had to go home. He said he could feel a migraine coming on.'

'What a shame,' Jordan said, thinking to herself that she wished she'd thought of that. Then she could have fled this extremely difficult scenario.

Running away from difficult scenarios,

however, had never been Jordan's style. She liked to face things head-on.

Which was hardly what she was doing at this moment.

It took an effort of will, but she finally turned her eyes back to meet Gino's.

'And who's this, Frank?' she asked coolly, and watched with some satisfaction as Gino's shoulders stiffened.

But no way was she going to give him the opportunity to say anything embarrassing in front of her boss. And he might, if she admitted to already knowing him.

'An extremely valuable new client,' Frank replied pompously. 'Mr Gino Bortelli, CEO of Bortelli Constructions, one of Melbourne's finest building companies. Henry helped him out last week with a contract.'

Ahh, so that was how he came to be here. Jordan wondered if someone had mentioned her name whilst he'd been here, signing that contract.

No, that couldn't be right. Gino hadn't even known she was a lawyer last Friday night, let alone where she worked.

'Hopefully, Gino will do Stedley & Parkinson the honour of letting us represent him in all his future business dealings in Sydney,' Frank added.

Jordan was used to Frank sucking up to wealthy clients, but he seemed to be outdoing himself this time.

'Unfortunately Henry called in sick at the last moment,' he swept on, before Jordan—or Gino—could say a single word. 'So I've been introducing Mr Bortelli to everyone. Jordan's one of our finest young litigators, Gino. She's gained quite a reputation during the few short years she's been with us.'

'Don't flatter me, Frank. How do you do, Mr Bortelli?' Jordan said, but refrained from holding out her hand.

'Very well, thank you,' Gino replied with a cool nod.

'I'll leave you in Jordan's good hands. I seem to recall Kerry has seated you next to each other. But don't get any ideas, Gino. Our Jordan has recently become engaged. To Chad Stedley,' he threw over his shoulder as he turned away. 'Our senior partner's son and heir.'

'Congratulations,' Gino said, his tone polite but his coldly contemptuous eyes spearing into her very soul.

Jordan could not help the guilty colour stealing into her cheeks. Luckily, Frank had turned away, and was already showing other guests to their seats around the table.

'So, is this the way we're going to play it tonight, Jordan?' Gino went on caustically. 'Like we're total strangers?'

Jordan gave him a long, cold look of her own. 'Everyone is sitting down for dinner, Mr Bortelli. I suggest we do the same. This way…'

He followed her round to the far side of the table, where she indicated his seat, right next to hers. Fortunately, nobody made any move to remove the place-settings on either side of them, meaning their conversation would not be easily overheard. Also fortunately, Kerry was seated to the left of Frank, on the same side of the table as Jordan, which meant she wouldn't witness any telling interplay between Jordan and Gino.

Once they'd settled in their chairs and the entrées had been served—tempura prawns on a salad base—Jordan decided to stop playing word games and cut to the chase.

'You're being here tonight is not a coincidence, is it?'

'My hiring Stedley & Parkinson as my legal representative was a coincidence.'

'But you knew I'd be here tonight?'

'Yes.'

Jordan's frustration level rose. 'Care to elaborate on that?'

'No.'

Jordan tried to think. Gino had always had difficulty taking no for an answer. She'd rejected him last Friday night. Had he had her investigated, perhaps? Found out where she worked? Found out about Chad?

She wouldn't put it past him.

'It must be difficult for you,' Gino said quietly, 'with your fiancé overseas. You must miss him.'

Jordan's heart lurched. 'How do you know that Chad's overseas?'

'Maybe Frank told me.'

'He didn't, though, did he? You've had me investigated.'

'My, my, what a suspicious mind you have. Must come from being a lawyer.'

'What is it that you want of me, Gino?'

He put down his entrée fork and slanted a smile her way.

It was a wickedly provocative smile—one which set her heart racing. And not from anger.

'What I've always wanted when I'm around you, Jordan,' he murmured, his sexy black eyes suddenly going from arctic cold to tropical heat.

When her hand began to tremble, she too put down her fork. Jerking her eyes away from his, she picked up her wine glass, gripping the stem tightly as she lifted it to her lips and swallowed a deep gulp.

The action allowed her to recover her composure a little. But her heart was still thudding loudly behind her ribs.

Finally, she turned her head to face him, her expression firm.

'I did not become engaged till after last Friday night,' she told him.

'And you think that exonerates you?' he muttered under his breath. 'You called me a liar and a cheat, Jordan. Yet all the while *you* were the liar and the cheat. I know exactly what happened last Friday night. You thought you could have your little bit of Italian rough whilst your wealthy lover was away. But when you found out I wasn't who you thought I was, you panicked and did a flit. But not before you dumped a whole lot of guilt on me. You even called me a coward. No one calls me a coward, Jordan, and gets away with it.'

Jordan's head spun with his vicious attack.

But Gino wasn't finished yet.

'What would happen, do you think, if I told your precious Chad what you were up to while he was away? I doubt you'd be wearing that ring for long. Or working here at good old Stedley & Parkinson's. They're a rather old-fashioned firm, aren't they?'

Once again all the blood drained from Jordan's face. It was as well she was sitting down. Shaken, she picked up her wine glass again and took another swallow, giving herself some more time to regroup. Finally, she put down the glass and picked up her fork.

'So this is what tonight's about, is it?' she bit out, spearing another prawn. 'Revenge. How typically Italian.'

'Indeed,' he agreed. 'You would have done well to remember that when you wounded my pride and my sense of honour.'

'You call it honourable to have me investigated?'

'A man has to do what a man has to do.'

'And what do you have to do, Gino?'

'I have to be with you again, Jordan,' he said, his voice vibrating with the most seductive passion. 'Tonight.'

Jordan only just stopped herself from gasping with shock. Instead, she lanced Gino with a dagger-like glare.

'Dream on, buster. Look, I told you last Friday night, and now I'm telling you again: it's over between us—has been for ten years. Last Friday was a big mistake on my part.'

Gino smiled a coolly confident smile. 'If you don't do as I ask, I will inform your beloved fiancé of what happened last Friday night. Somehow I don't think it will rate with him that, technically, you weren't engaged at the time.'

'Why, you ba—'

'Hush,' he broke in swiftly. 'You wouldn't want dear old Frank hearing you swear at such a valuable new client, would you?'

Jordan shot him another savage glare before

grabbing her wine glass again, and emptying it down her throat with a speed which had several pairs of eyes glancing her way across the table in surprise.

She never drank much at these company dinners. Never did anything which anyone could call remotely reckless, let alone wicked.

Jordan knew Gino's ultimatum was wicked. And without care for her future well-being. His wanting her was strictly sexual, his desire made stronger by his need to strip her not just of her clothes, but her pride.

But, despite all that, Jordan had the dreadful suspicion that in the end she would go along with what he wanted—not to keep him silent, but because, down deep, she *wanted* to spend the night with him.

That had to be wicked. *She* had to be wicked.

Either that, or she was still in love with Gino.

But how could she love a man who would do such an appalling thing as try to blackmail her into bed?

No, this wasn't love which was making her blood roar like red-hot lava around her veins. This was lust. A lust so exciting and so powerful she had no chance of resisting it.

Sexually, she was putty in his hands. Always had been. Always would be.

At the same time, she could not allow Gino to suspect her weakness. That would be setting herself up as a perfect victim for his voracious carnal appetite. Safety lay in letting him think that she despised him for doing to her.

Though she wasn't at all sure that she did. His daring excited her almost as much as his desire.

God, but she was hopeless where he was concerned.

Thank heavens she'd perfected the art of steely composure to cover any inner nerves.

'Blackmailers are notorious for never being satisfied,' she said curtly. 'If I do as you want, what's to stop you demanding more after tonight is over?'

'I give you my word that if you spend tonight with me I will go home to Melbourne in the morning and never bother you again.'

'Pardon me if I don't put much store in your word.'

'What alternative do you have?'

'I could tell Chad what happened last Friday. He might understand.'

'*I* wouldn't,' Gino growled.

And neither would Chad, Jordan conceded.

'It's not too much to ask, is it?' Gino went on. 'One night with me, in exchange for a lifetime as Mrs Chad Stedley.'

'What's to stop you causing trouble in my marriage at some future date?' she asked curtly.

'Nothing—other than my word. But I presume once you're married you will move to New York. As much as I'm going to enjoy having you at my beck and call tonight, I doubt I'd travel that far for a repeat performance.'

'Does your family know that you're a heartless, conscienceless bastard?'

His face darkened. 'Leave my family out of this.'

'Gladly.'

'So, what's your answer, Jordan?' he snapped. 'Do we have a deal or not?'

Jordan grimaced, then gritted her teeth. Why was it just him who could make her heart race like this? Who could make her forget her pride? Could make her crave the things he did to her?

It infuriated her that she was so weak with him when normally she was a strong person, with a mind of her own. If it was any other man she would tell him to go to hell. There again, if it had been any other man she would not have willingly had sex with him last Friday night.

'You do realise I will hate you for ever for doing this?' she grated out under her breath.

'It'll be worth it,' he returned coldly.

What would be worth it? she wondered, and worried.

An image popped into her mind, that of herself standing naked in front of him last

Friday night and swearing that he would never see her like that again.

Bold, brave, foolish words. Words which Gino was obviously determined to make her regret.

The waiter taking away their empty entrée plates put paid to any conversation for a short while. The second of their crystal wine glasses was filled. Still white, but a Chardonnay this time, instead of the crisp Chablis which had accompanied the seafood cocktail. Clearly the main course was going to be something light.

'I should tell you to go to hell,' Jordan bit out, once the waiters had moved away from them.

'You should, but you won't. You'll do what I want.'

'Don't be so sure.'

'But I am. Because I'm not the only one here who's heartless and conscienceless. Not to mention ambitious. Oh, yes, let's not forget ambitious.'

'You know nothing about the woman I am.'

'Neither do I want to. I might have once. But I now prefer to keep my knowledge of you to the biblical kind. So is it a deal, Mrs Stedley-to-be? Will you trade total surrender of your body tonight in exchange for my silence?'

'*Total* surrender?' she repeated, aghast and aroused at the same time.

'Didn't I mention that?'

'No,' she said, shaken by the level of her sexual excitement.

'I will not ask you to do anything you haven't done with me before,' he said.

Jordan suppressed a groan. That didn't leave much, if anything at all. Her sex-life with Chad had never been as adventurous as it had been with Gino. Not even remotely.

'You have ten seconds to seal this deal,' he said, with chilling finality, 'or I will do what I said I would. Immediately. I have your fiancé's personal phone number in the menu of my cell-phone. A simple visit to the gents will give me the opportunity to call him right now.'

Jordan would have called his bluff if he'd been any other man.

But she knew Gino meant it.

'In that case,' she said, her stomach contracting as she tried to imagine the consequences of Gino's appalling ultimatum. 'It's a deal.'

# CHAPTER TEN

WHEN she agreed, it confirmed to Gino what he'd suspected all week: the sweet, sensual, sincere girl he'd once known and loved had turned into a cold-blooded, gold-digging bitch.

She didn't love Chad Stedley. How could she when she'd gone to bed with *him* last Friday night?

But she was wearing Stedley's engagement ring.

Gino had been furious when he found out she was engaged.

No, furious didn't do his emotions justice; he'd been absolutely livid.

He'd come here tonight without any definite plan in mind. He'd just wanted to look her in the eye and let her know that he knew what kind of woman she was. But the moment he'd set eyes on her, standing there with her back to him, looking sexy in that prim little black dress, desire had consumed every pore in his body. By the time she turned round, he'd hated her for the way she could make him crave her, despite everything.

Blackmailing her into bed had not been on his agenda, however, till she'd added insult to injury by arrogantly pretending she didn't know him.

That had been the moment when he'd resolved to bring her down a peg or two. To use her own ruthless ambition against her, at the same time satisfying his own rapidly escalating desire.

Even so, he'd still been shocked when she'd agreed to his proposal. Shocked and stirred. Right now, he was so turned on it would have been embarrassing if he hadn't been sitting at a table.

'I hope you're happy now,' she muttered.

Happy? No, he wasn't happy. How could be

happy when the only reason she was going to go to bed with him was so that she could marry someone else?

Or was that really the case?

A sidewards glance showed him that her face was flushed. Was that anger, or the same kind of excitement currently heating his own blood?

The sexual chemistry between them had once been electric. That chemistry had still been there last Friday night. There was no reason to believe that had changed just because she'd found out he wasn't who she thought he was.

Jordan might hate him, but underneath her hatred lay a desire as insidious and as irresistible as his own for her.

Gino could not wait to have her to himself—to have her stand naked for him the way she'd said she never would again—to have her do all the things he'd taught her ten years ago.

The main course arriving only slightly

soothed the primitive passions which had begun boiling up within him.

The waiter announced that it was grilled Barramundi, served with a tomato and cucumber salsa, along with baked sweet potato and a fresh garden salad.

Gino fell to eating the meal with gusto. His appetite was always good when his testosterone was up and running.

Jordan, he noticed, just picked at her food. But she drank plenty of wine.

Good, he thought. She was even sexier when she was tipsy, and beautifully co-operative. Or she'd used to be.

'When?' she suddenly whispered.

He did not turn his head to speak.

'When, what?' he muttered, then forked some more of the mouthwatering fish between his lips.

'When does all this begin? And where?'

He let her wait for his answer till he'd savoured the fish, then swallowed.

'As soon as we can get away from here. I've

booked a suite at the Regency. One of their themed honeymoon suites.'

He could feel her eyes burning into him.

'How could you?' she breathed.

'How could I what?'

'Book a honeymoon suite.'

In actual fact he hadn't booked the honeymoon suite with any ulterior motive. He certainly hadn't imagined Jordan would be sharing it with him when he had. But the Regency was having a huge convention there this weekend. The only rooms available had been a couple of the honeymoon suites. Gino hadn't thought to book in advance, and couldn't be bothered going to another hotel.

But he wasn't going to tell her that. Clearly his booking a suite had struck a nerve with her.

Good.

'It's called the French Bordello suite,' he told her with a devilish smile. 'I thought it rather appropriate.'

Jordan shook her head at him.

'You really are wicked.'

'And what are you, Jordan?' he countered coldly. 'An innocent?'

'No,' she agreed. 'If I was, I wouldn't have anything to do with you.'

I should have told him to go to hell, Jordan groaned silently as she dropped her eyes back to her plate.

Gino's blackmailing her into bed was bad enough. His booking a honeymoon suite was so insensitive that it bordered on sadism. Surely he must know she'd once have given anything to share a honeymoon suite with him? Becoming Mrs Gino Bortelli had been her ultimate dream.

Becoming Gino Bortelli's mistress for one night was more like a nightmare.

Yet the prospect excited her unbearably.

Her hands shook when she picked up her knife and fork, her stomach churning so much that she simply could not eat.

Gino could, she noticed bitterly. And so could

everyone else. But it was no use. Her appetite was gone. Putting her cutlery down, she picked up her wine glass and sipped it slowly.

'No wonder you're thin,' Gino said. 'You don't eat.'

Jordan ignored him and continued sipping her wine. But it wasn't long before she began to feel light-headed, so she put the glass down, picked up her fork and forced a few mouthfuls of the meal down past the lump in her throat.

'That's better,' Gino said, and she threw him a sour glare.

'It's a wonder I can eat at all, with what's ahead of me tonight.'

'Really? When I'm excited I eat all the more.'

'How can you possibly enjoy going to bed with a woman who hates you?'

'That's one thing you should learn about men, Jordan. They do not have to love or even like their sexual partner to enjoy themselves in bed.'

'You do realise that what you're going to do tonight is tantamount to coercion?'

'Oh, come now, Jordan. Coercion?' A dry laugh broke from his lips. 'I'll remind you that you said that when you beg me for more.'

Jordan sucked in sharply, both at his arrogance and at the hot wave of desire which suddenly flooded her body.

Still, after what he'd just said Jordan finally accepted that Gino had never loved her at all. She'd just been a sex object to him, a plaything.

What he'd loved about her was being able to take her virgin body and turn her into his ultimate fantasy female. Their affair had had nothing to do with love, it had just been sex.

Last Friday night had been more of the same. And so would tonight.

Jordan's thoughts hardened her heart to him, but it didn't dampen her desire. She still wanted to be with him, and the disgusting realisation was making her hate herself almost as much as him.

'You have no soul,' she muttered.

'Then we're well matched,' he countered.

'Why don't you stop talking and just let me eat?'

'Be my guest.'

Each mouthful felt like swill, but it was better to eat than to drink, or—heaven forbid—get into some destructive repartee with Gino.

By the time the waiter came round to remove her plate—everyone else had finished their meal by then—Jordan had managed to consume a reasonable amount, washed down with two full glasses of wine.

Frank standing up and toasting all their new clients was a welcome distraction. But she wasn't so keen when he also toasted her success with the Johnson case this week. It reminded her that there wouldn't be too many similar successes for her in the near future.

Not at Stedley & Parkinson.

Her allowing Gino to blackmail her into bed with him meant the death of her life here—because it meant the death of her engagement to Chad.

She could not in all conscience spend tonight at Gino's sexual beck and call, then go on to marry Chad; he deserved better than that.

Which meant she would have to call him tomorrow and break off their engagement, as well as resign from Stedley & Parkinson on Monday.

For how could she go on working here under those circumstances? Better that she get out now, with her reputation still intact. She would tell Frank that the pressure of the job and the distress of her broken engagement was too much, and that she needed a break from working. That way she could leave with proper references.

Maybe she'd treat herself to a holiday somewhere far far away.

Not Italy, though. China, perhaps. Somewhere different.

As she sat there, making plans, her mind reluctantly returned to Chad. He was going to be very annoyed with her. But he would survive.

Jordan comforted herself with the thought that they hadn't shared a grand passion.

'Have you set a date for your wedding?' Gino suddenly asked, snapping her back to the reality of where she was and whom she was sitting next to.

She turned cold eyes his way. 'I thought I said I didn't want to talk.'

'Better than sitting here twiddling our thumbs.'

'I don't agree.'

'I hope it's not a shotgun wedding?'

'What? Don't be ridiculous.'

'Why is it ridiculous? Stedley's a very good catch. You wouldn't be the first girl to snare herself a wealthy husband with pregnancy.'

'I earn a very good salary. I don't need a wealthy husband.'

'You know the famous saying: you can never be too rich or too thin.'

'Can we terminate this conversation, please?'

'Fine. But I must ask one thing before we have sex tonight.'

Jordan winced at Gino's verbalising of what they would be doing later. Not for the first time tonight she thanked heaven no one could overhear their conversation. The empty seats on either side of them had been a godsend—as was the very convenient arrangement of flowers sitting between them and the people opposite.

'What is it?' she said with an irritable sigh.

'Does Chad wear a condom when he has sex with you?' Gino asked.

'Do *you* use a condom when you sleep with your girlfriend?' she shot back.

'Always. Now answer the question.'

Jordan didn't want to, but she could see no way out.

'Yes,' she admitted.

'I thought he might.'

Jordan blinked. 'Why do you say it like that?'

'Like what?'

'Like you think Chad's sleeping around on me.'

'Well, you're sleeping around on him.'

'Last Friday night was the one and only time.'

'What about tonight?'

'You can't possibly count tonight. You're forcing me.'

'Ahh, yes. So I am,' he said, but his tone was sarcastic, as though he knew full well she was more than willing.

Jordan closed her eyes against this most terrible truth. What kind of person was she to do this? Okay, so she was going to break her engagement. That, at least, was the right thing to do. But she was still going to spend the night with a man who didn't care for her, and who had a girlfriend back in Melbourne.

Both of them were technically being unfaithful to their partners.

Gino was right. She was just as bad as he was.

When she opened her eyes again her dessert was sitting in front of her—some kind of chocolate concoction, with swirls of cream and berries decorating the plate. The waiter had also refilled her wine glass.

She reached for it first, hoping to drown her scruples with alcohol. Gino, she noted out of the corner of her eyes, was already eating his dessert. By the time she picked up her dessert fork he'd finished.

'Do you intend working after you've become Mrs Chad Stedley?'

Jordan sighed again. She wished she could tell Gino to shut up, in no uncertain terms, but she doubted he would comply.

'I will never give up working,' she told him, her tone curt.

'Not even when you have a baby?'

Jordan gritted her teeth. 'Not even then.'

'Do you want children?'

Jordan hated the way her heart lurched. 'What business is that of yours?' she snapped. *He* didn't want to marry her, or have children by her. All he wanted was to have sex with her.

'Just curious.'

'Don't be. We made a deal. And it only

includes access to my body. Not my soul. Or my goals. Now, if you don't mind, I would like to leave this topic of conversation alone for the rest of this dinner. I've agreed to what you wanted. Be happy with that.'

'I won't be happy till you're in my arms again.'

Jordan smothered a groan. Why did he have to say things like that? And why did she have to respond so mindlessly?

She closed her eyes, thinking that happiness would never be hers again. Not if she did this. Being with Gino again would destroy her. She could feel it already—the disintegration of her will, the longing to surrender herself to him. It was insidious, this power he had over her. She could feel it, radiating out from him, drawing her into his spell.

Jordan put down her fork, knowing that this time she would not be able to force herself to eat a single bite.

'Men like you should be castrated,' she muttered.

Gino laughed softly. 'Then what would women like you do?'

'Have some peace in their lives.'

'How boring that sounds. At least you won't be bored tonight. You're going to feel more alive than you have in years.'

'And you, Gino? What will you feel?'

He smiled at her. 'You do like cross-examining people, don't you? My feelings will be my own. I don't share them with women who hate me.'

'Yet you expect me to share your bed? How perverse is that?'

'Extremely perverse,' he whispered as he leant towards her, his breath warmth against her ear. 'I will think about your hatred when you stand naked before me. And when you beg me to do it to you—as you will, Jordan my sweet. Because I know that part of you through and through. I know your secret needs and desires. You might hate me, but down deep, in that place reserved for the darkest of truths, you want me as much as I want you. No. Perhaps not *that* much. Here—give me your hand and see what you've already done to me.'

Jordan stiffened in the chair when he took her hand and pulled it into his lap, pressing it against him.

'Stop that,' she hissed as she snatched her hand away. 'I will not be humiliated by you, Gino. You will treat me with respect. If you cross the line of decency just once, the deal's off. I'll tell Chad myself I had a one-night stand with an old boyfriend and take my chances. Do I make myself clear?'

'Perfectly.'

'I have no intention of leaving this dinner with you, either. I will go to the Regency independently. Leave my name and a spare key card for me at Reception.'

'But they'll think you're a paid whore if I do that!' he protested.

'They wouldn't be far wrong, then, would they?'

Gino scowled. 'I'll tell them that my wife will be joining me after a late flight from Melbourne.'

'No,' Jordan snapped. 'I will not pretend to be your wife.'

'You've become very stubborn.'

'I'm an adult woman now, Gino, not a silly young girl.'

'I preferred the silly young girl,' he said, his expression still disgruntled.

'I'm sure you did. So the deal's off, is it? You don't want me any more now that you've discovered the stubborn new me?'

He stared into her eyes for a long moment. 'Stop trying to pick a fight with me, Jordan. You and I both know that neither of us wants that. Now eat your dessert; it's delicious.'

'I can't eat any more,' she said, and pushed the plate away.

'You need taking in hand, woman. Which I will take pleasure in doing as soon as this dinner is over.'

'In your dreams,' she snapped.

'No. In the French Bordello suite at the Regency. In a four-poster bed. All night long.'

# CHAPTER ELEVEN

JORDAN was standing at the window behind her desk, staring blankly down at the city, when her office door opened.

'I thought I'd find you here,' Kerry said.

Jordan turned and smiled a small smile at her friend. 'Why's that?'

'Because you're in some kind of antisocial mood. You couldn't wait to get out of that dinner, could you?'

'I didn't have much of an appetite tonight,' Jordan said.

'The food was good, though, wasn't it?'

'Very good.' Jordan glanced at her watch. She would have to be leaving soon. Gino had warned her not to be late, and he'd already been gone ten minutes.

'How did you get on with Mr Bortelli?'

'What?' Jordan looked up. 'Oh, not too bad. He liked the food.'

'He didn't make a pass at you, did he?'

Jordan stiffened. 'Why on earth would you say that?'

'Just a feeling. You seem…agitated.'

For a split second Jordan was tempted to tell Kerry everything. But she just couldn't.

'I'm still strung up after last week. The Johnson case was rather draining. I…I might take a break from work shortly.'

'You know, I think that would be a good idea. Why don't you surprise Chad by flying over to the States?'

Jordan shook her head. 'No. I don't want to do that.'

'You're not having second thoughts about marrying him, are you?'

Jordan swallowed. 'Actually, I am.'

'Oh, Jordan,' Kerry said, her face falling.

'Yes, I know. I'm a fool. Probably a bigger

fool than you realise.' Suddenly tears filled Jordan's eyes. She had to get out of here, and fast. Blinking madly, she wrenched open her desk drawer and retrieved her purse from where she'd left it earlier.

When she lifted her eyes back to Kerry's she had herself under control again. 'I need to go home and get a good night's sleep. See you on Monday.'

'Look after yourself,' Kerry called after her as she hurried from the office.

No one was in the lift on the ride down, giving Jordan the perfect opportunity to slip off her engagement ring and pop it into the zippered section of her purse.

No way could she wear Chad's ring whilst she was with Gino. He wouldn't allow it, anyway.

The security man in the foyer asked Jordan if she wanted him to call her a taxi. The Regency was a relatively short walk away— only a couple of blocks. But on a Saturday

night any walk in the city could be danger-
ous—especially for a woman on her own.

Jordan would normally have taken a taxi, but
not this time.

She welcomed the cool night air outside,
welcomed the risk.

If someone mugged her or accosted her, then
it was only what she deserved.

Of course no one did either, and she was
pushing her way through the revolving glass
doors of the hotel's entrance in less than ten
minutes. By then her heart was pounding
behind her ribs and her face felt flushed.
Another glance at her watch showed that it
was only just after ten-thirty.

Her stiletto heels clacked on the marble floor
of the arcade as she hurried along it—past the
bouncer who stood at the doorway to the
Rendezvous bar, past the bistro and the bou-
tiques. The arcade led into the hotel foyer
proper, and the reception desk was on her left.

Jordan hated that she'd have to deal with a male desk clerk. She'd been hoping for a woman.

'Ahh, yes…Ms Gray,' he said, with a knowing little smirk on his fleshy lips as he handed her the key card. 'Mr Bortelli said you were to go right up. The French Bordello suite is on the twelfth floor.'

'Thank you,' she replied coolly, hoping her cheeks weren't as red as they felt.

The ride up to the twelfth floor felt surreal, with her conflicting emotions threatening to overwhelm her. Her brain kept telling her not to do this. She could still turn round and go home. But her body refused to obey.

Before she knew it she was standing in front of the door which had *French Bordello Suite* marked on it in gold letters.

Should she knock, or let herself in?

Her right hand balled into a fist as she lifted it to knock.

A few short but agonising seconds passed before the door was wrenched open.

Gino stood there, his black eyes glowering impatience at her. He'd taken off his jacket, she noted, and the bow-tie. He'd also opened the top button of his white dress-shirt.

'You took your time,' he grumbled.

'I walked.'

'You what?' he snapped, then grabbed her hand and pulled her inside, kicking the door shut with his foot. 'What kind of risk-taker are you, woman?'

Jordan could have told him, in no uncertain terms, but decided not to say a word. Instead, she yanked her hand out of his, and was about to head further into the room when she ground to a halt.

'Good heavens!' she exclaimed.

Jordan just stood there, shaking her head at the over-the-top décor. Had the designer copied rooms in a real French Bordello? she wondered. Or simply come up with what a French Bordello might be like in his or her imagination?

The colours were too rich for Jordan's taste,

the furniture way too ornate. At the same time there was no denying that whoever had designed this place had created a decadent, sensual atmosphere: dark red-coloured carpet on the floor, wood-panelled walls, two gold brocade-covered sofas, with elaborately carved legs. Marble-topped tables, gold velvet drapes at the window, subdued lighting from heavily fringed lamps whose bases were brass figurines of naked women.

The bedroom was separated from the sitting area by double doors, currently open, giving Jordan a glimpse of the bottom half of the four-poster bed Gino had mentioned. In there the colours were reversed—the carpet gold and the walls covered in a deep red wallpaper, the velvet drapes around the bed the same dark red colour.

'Does that mean you like it or not?' Gino said drily by her side.

'It's not exactly my cup of tea,' she replied.

'Wait till you see the bathroom.'

A stab of nervous tension suddenly set her

bladder on edge. 'I think I need to go see it right now.'

'Be my guest,' Gino invited.

'Alone,' she added sharply.

No television, she noted as she hurried through the sitting room, nor a mini-bar. Though there was an antique cabinet in one corner which could have hidden anything. A bottle of French champagne—already opened—sat in a silver ice bucket on the marble-topped coffee table, along with some tasty little treats: strawberries…caviar… And—if she wasn't mistaken—chocolate truffles.

Was that Gino's doing? Or the hotel's?

The bedroom was as sumptuous as it looked from a distance. The bedspread was made of red and gold quilted satin, the pillows of gold satin, as were the sheets. The brass bases of the bedside lamps were more naked ladies in various poses. An elegant glass bottle stood next to one lamp, filled with what looked like a body lotion of some kind.

The bathroom lived up to Gino's warning: black marble dominated the room, covering the floors, walls and ceiling. The twin sink units were made of the same marble, the bowls as well. The toilet, bidet and corner spa bath were in a rich cream colour, the taps and other fittings gold-plated. The towels were scarlet, as were the floor mats. Several small alcoves had been carved high up in the marble walls. Tonight they held gold candles which were lit, looking like glow-worms in a dark cave—a dark, sexually charged cave.

Jordan could only imagine what Gino had in mind for that room later on. She shuddered anew as she washed her hands at the sink, grateful that the dim light wouldn't let her see the excitement in her eyes reflected in the mirror.

She combed her slightly breeze-blown hair, but didn't bother to refresh her lipstick. What was the point? It wouldn't be there for long.

Gathering herself, she exited the bathroom and returned to the sitting area, where Gino was standing at the window with his back to her. He turned at the sound of her entry. He was holding a near full glass of champagne, and he was frowning.

'I've been thinking,' he began.

'Yes?'

'I was wrong to blackmail you into this. It's not what I intended to do when I went to that dinner tonight. It's not what I want.'

Jordan had never been so astounded in all her life.

'What is it that you want, then?'

'I still want you, Jordan. That hasn't changed. But I want you to come to me willingly. I don't want to force you, or even to seduce you. I want what we once had together. You—eager to surrender yourself to me. I don't want you to hate me in the morning. And I don't want to hate myself.'

Jordan just stared at Gino, his amazing and highly unexpected turnaround bringing a fierce frustration which found its voice in anger.

'I don't think you know what you want, Gino,' she said sharply. 'Look, if it makes you feel any better, then I *have* come here willingly. It's not because you blackmailed me. You have some kind of hold over me. I admit it. You turn up out of the blue, crook your finger, and silly Jordan comes running. But don't delude yourself into thinking we can recapture what we once had. For one thing, I don't love you any more. How could I possibly love a man who has me investigated behind my back? But, yes, I still lust after you. You were right in what you said at that table tonight. You know what I like. You know all my dark little secrets.

'So here I am,' she added, reaching up behind her back and pulling the zipper down. 'Doing what I vowed I'd never do. But not because of your threat to tell Chad. I'm hoping that once I've had my fill of you tonight I'll be able to walk away in the morning and make a decent life for myself with a man who cares about me and wants to marry me.'

\* \* \*

Gino watched, appalled but cripplingly aroused, as she peeled her dress off her shoulders and let it fall to the floor, leaving her standing there in her underwear.

Not prim and proper underwear, but sexy underwear. A black satin teddy, with suspenders attached to shiny flesh-coloured stockings.

Her glittering blue eyes held his boldly whilst she kicked off her shoes and then unflicked each suspender. With a haughty toss of her lovely blonde hair she moved over to the coffee table and put one foot up, rolling the stocking down to her toes before snapping it off.

Gino's gut crunched down hard at the thought that she might have performed like this for Stedley. Though if she had, then what was she doing here?

*No, it's only with me that she's like this. She's virtually said as much.*

The other stocking followed, then the pearls, which she tossed aside as carelessly as the nylons. When she hooked her fingers under the thin satin straps of the teddy Gino's stopped breathing altogether. His blood, however, was still roaring round his veins, engorging his flesh to titanic proportions.

She actually smiled as she peeled the garment down her body. A slow siren's smile.

'Don't look so gobsmacked,' she said, when she finally stood there in the nude. 'This is what you wanted, isn't it?'

Gino's hand gripped the stem of his glass with such force that it was a miracle it didn't snap.

'No,' he ground out. 'Not quite. Put the shoes back on.'

Now it was her turn to look gobsmacked.

'That's the way I pictured you when I was eating dinner tonight. That's what I want. For starters,' he added, all qualms gone over how he was going to treat her tonight. He'd tried to do the right thing, but she wanted none of it. *This* was what she wanted. To have her fill of him. And he was more than happy to oblige!

* * *

Jordan swallowed, her throat suddenly dry. She should never have started stripping in front of him, never have taken him on.

It had only been a matter of time before her recklessness backfired on her.

Gino no longer looked shocked. His expression was cold and implacable.

'Do it!' he ordered.

Jordan's feet found her shoes. The height of the heels changed the way she stood. The sharp angle of her feet made her straighten her shoulders and suck in her stomach, those actions thrusting her breasts forward and upwards.

Gino's black eyes narrowed as he looked her up and down, his heavily hooded gaze as hard as it was exciting.

Had he known she would feel different standing there in the nude with her high heels on? More exposed? More…aroused?

Yes, of course he knew. He knew she was standing there, trembling inside with anticipation of what would come next. Knew that she thrilled to his commands and his demands.

'That's better,' he said, a dark triumph in his eyes. 'Now come over here…'

# CHAPTER TWELVE

JORDAN walked slowly towards him, each step bringing a heightened awareness of her female body.

By the time she stood before him her lips had fallen apart and her heartbeat had quickened, her chest rising and falling, her belly stretched tight with tension.

'Here,' he said, and held his glass to her lips. 'You look like you could do with a drink.'

He tipped up the glass and watched her drink it all down.

The champagne fizzed into her stomach, her head spinning—but not because of the alcohol.

Jordan could not recall ever being this excited. Or this mesmerised. This was different from ten years ago. Different from last Friday night.

Tonight, she accepted dazedly, was going to be an experience which would change her life for ever.

When he tossed the empty glass onto one of the sofas, then ran the back of his right hand across the hard tips of her breasts, a violent tremor rippled down her spine.

'Do you know how sexy you look?' he murmured, as he trailed his fingers down over her tautly held stomach. 'But you'd look even sexier if you moved your legs apart a little.'

When she just blinked, he smiled a rather cold smile. 'I thought we'd agreed on total surrender for tonight? Total surrender means doing as you're told when you're told. Of course if you've changed your mind about wanting your fill of me, that's your choice. Get dressed and leave. I won't stop you. But if you decide to stay, then we do things my way.'

The ruthlessness in his voice shocked her. But it turned her on at the same time.

'You seem to have lost your tongue,' he went on. 'But, since you're still here, I take it you agree with my conditions for tonight?'

Jordan swallowed, then licked her parched lips.

'That too,' he said, his coal-black eyes fixed on her mouth. 'But later—after we've had a relaxing bath. You stay right where you are till I run the water.'

'Gino—no,' she choked out, her excitement already at fever pitch.

'No, what?' he shot back.

'Don't leave me like this. I can't bear it.'

He glared at her with something akin to hatred. But then his eyes dissolved in a blaze of molten desire. With a tortured groan he caught her to him, his arms enfolding her into a rough embrace, his mouth brutal in its possession of hers.

She melted against him with a naked moan, glorying in the savagery of his kiss. If he'd been tender with her she might have started crying. This way she could lose herself in his wild passion, as well as her own.

The buttons on his shirt were pressing painfully into her chest. But she didn't care. She welcomed the pain…and the madness.

Soon his tongue in her mouth wasn't enough. She needed him inside her. Needed to be filled as only he had ever filled her.

Somehow she freed her mouth from his, her breathing like a marathon runner nearing the end of a race.

'Do it to me,' she cried.

His eyes glowered down at her, then glittered in a way which sent a shiver running down her spine. 'Here?'

'Yes,' she practically sobbed.

He grabbed her by the waist and lifted her off her feet, turning her round and carrying her over to the floor-length window. There, he stood her in the centre of it, her bottom and shoulders pressed up against the cool glass.

Jordan gasped when he lifted her arms upwards and outwards.

'Take hold of the curtains,' he ordered her. 'And don't let go.'

Her hands trembled as they clasped the edges of the velvet swags. What must she look like, standing there like some pagan sacrifice? Could she be seen from the windows of the building opposite? Were people watching them?

'Move your legs further apart,' Gino ordered, as he stripped off his shirt and tossed it aside.

Jordan closed her eyes, then did as she was told. Her hands clutched tighter at the velvet, so tight that it was a wonder she didn't bring the curtains down around her.

The sudden feel of Gino's breath on her face had her eyelids fluttering back open.

'I want you to watch, my love,' he murmured, leaning down to run his tongue-tip around her startled mouth. 'And to witness. Everything.'

'I…I am not your love,' she cried, shuddering when one his hands slipped between her legs.

'You are tonight.'

'No,' she denied, even as she trembled with desire.

'This tells me differently,' he murmured against her panting mouth. 'This tells me that tonight you *are* mine.'

His eyes held hers as his hand continued with its most devastatingly intimate exploration. Jordan tried to fight the feelings his skilful touch evoked, tried not to melt at his watching her like that. But it was a futile effort. Her whole body stiffened as it rushed towards a climax.

Gino's abandoning her barely a breath before her release brought a perverse cry of protest.

'Patience,' he growled, and went back to undressing in front of her.

Jordan's shoulders sagged, her upper arms beginning to ache. But the sight of Gino naked had her spine straightening again.

'You like what you see?' he taunted as he came back to her.

Jordan could no longer speak. She just wanted him inside her. She didn't care who might be watching them—didn't care about anything but his flesh filling hers.

It did. Quite roughly. Surging up into her body with such force that she was momentarily lifted off the floor. His hands lifted to press against the glass on either side of her head, his mouth grazing her hair as he thrust into her, his chest rubbing against the tips of her breasts.

Jordan had never experienced a coupling so passionate or so primitive. Not even with Gino himself, all those years ago.

It spun her out of her head, out of her body. She was there, but not there. Gino had said he wanted her to watch and to witness everything. That was exactly what it felt as if she was doing: being both participant and observer.

Is that really me there, spread naked against the window, keeping myself a willing captive for this man?

I am doomed, she thought hysterically. Doomed!

'Gino,' she cried out as she came. 'Oh, Gino…'

Gino heard her call out his name. Felt her flesh start spasming around his.

What little was left of his control shattered, his mind exploding along with his body, his thoughts spinning out into the stratosphere.

She had to still love him to let him do such things to her, he reasoned wildly in the heat of the moment. Had to. The girl he'd known all those years could not have changed that much.

And if she loved him, then she didn't love Stedley. She was just marrying him because she was getting older and wanted children. Women always wanted children.

*He* could give her children, if that was what she so desperately wanted. They could work something out—some arrangement: they could be lovers, or live together. He hadn't given any deathbed promise that he would not *live* with a girl who wasn't Italian.

Some common sense had returned, however, by the time she let go of the curtains and began to sag downwards.

She didn't necessarily have to love him to enjoy what he'd just done to her, he conceded, as he withdrew and scooped her up into his arms. She wasn't the same girl she'd been ten years ago. She'd changed.

*He'd* changed, hadn't he?

She'd told him how it was earlier: this was all about sex. A fatal-attraction kind of sex which had nothing to do with love, but with need: a dark, driving need which obsessed and possessed.

Gino gritted his teeth. He already felt obsessed and possessed.

Jordan had expressed the hope that one night with him would cure her of her need.

As Gino carried her into the bedroom he vowed to make sure that it did not.

# CHAPTER THIRTEEN

JORDAN shivered when Gino lowered her onto the cool satin quilt, goosebumps breaking out all over her body.

'I'll go run us that bath now,' he said, as he slipped off her shoes and then wrapped the quilt tightly around her.

'Don't go to sleep,' he added, giving her a soft peck on her forehead before heading for the bathroom.

Jordan stared after him, her slightly fuzzy mind at a loss to understand his sudden change of attitude. Where had the ruthless lover of a few moments ago gone? Was his tenderness for real? Or just a ploy to seduce her into further compliance?

'Won't be too long,' he said jauntily as he

walked back through the bedroom, returning with the ice bucket and two champagne glasses. A second trip out to the sitting room had him collecting the two plates of delicacies.

'Can't have you passing out from thirst and hunger, can I?' he remarked with a wicked smile as he headed back to the bathroom.

Any fuzziness in Jordan's head immediately cleared. Not true tenderness. A seductive ploy.

How silly of her to start hoping for anything different.

'All done!' he announced, on his third return to the bedroom. 'Just one more thing needed, my love. *You.*'

Jordan did her best not to swoon when he threw back the quilt, then scooped her up from the bed. But having her naked flesh held tight against Gino's was not conducive to calm.

The bathroom looked both romantic and decadent at the same time, what with the candles, the champagne and the spa filled to the brim with fragrant-smelling bubbles.

'You'd better put your hair up,' he suggested. 'Or it'll get wet.'

Jordan reached up to wrap her hair on top of her head in a knot, her eyes never leaving his.

'You are so beautiful,' he murmured, and kissed her lightly on the lips.

She blinked, then gasped when he went to step into the spa bath, still carrying her.

'Oh, do be careful.'

'I won't drop you,' he told her confidently. 'Don't worry.'

The water under the bubbles was deliciously warm, and Jordan sighed with relief when Gino finally sat down, angling her round so that she was sitting on his thighs, her back leaning against his.

'Comfy like that?' he asked.

Jordan swallowed. 'Are you?'

He laughed. 'I have a feeling I won't be soon. But I'll worry about that later. This is just like the old days, isn't it? We had plenty of baths together then.'

'I…I don't want to talk about the old days, Gino.'

'Fine. Here…have a sip of champagne,' he said, picking up one of the full glasses and holding it to her lips.

Jordan was about to blindly open her lips when a wave of rebellion struck. 'I'd rather have my own glass, thank you.'

'Okay. Take this one.'

He gave it to her, but didn't get the other glass for himself. Instead, he picked up the sea sponge which was lying on the bath's edge and rubbed it across her stomach.

When he moved it up to her breasts she gasped, spilling some champagne as she jerked away from Gino's chest.

'Relax,' he said, and used the sponge to press her back into her leaning position. 'You'll like it. I promise. Just lie back, sip your champagne, and keep your arms out of my way.'

It seemed silly to tell him to stop. Because of course she did like it—especially when the sponge grazed over her rock-hard nipples. Her pleasure was a double-edged sword, however, as her sexual tension increased with each passing moment. Soon every muscle she owned was twisted into a tight knot. She tried sipping more of the champagne, but nothing relaxed her for long.

'Tell me about that case you won,' Gino said.

Jordan turned her head and flicked startled eyes up at him.

'You…you can't be serious,' she choked out.

'Why not?' he returned.

'Because I can't think, let alone talk when you're doing that.'

'Yes, you can. Try it,' he said, moving the sponge down over her stomach again, then lower…

'Oh!' she cried as her hips bucked upwards.

'God, woman,' Gino growled.

When she felt his flesh suddenly slide up into her Jordan froze, gripping the champagne glass for dear life.

'Just relax now,' he advised again, as he eased her back down into a sitting position. 'Lie back and don't move. I want to hear about that case you won first.'

'How can I? I…I can't think.'

'You can, and you will.'

Jordan could not believe she was doing this. She was desperate to move, but he kept her still with his hands splayed across her stomach.

'What compensation did you get her in the end?' he asked, after she'd related the whole story to him.

'Three million.'

'A tidy sum.'

'Sharni still wasn't a happy woman. Because it wasn't about money, really. It was about justice. Money doesn't make people happy.'

'But it can help.'

'I suppose so.' She *so* wished he would stop talking.

'*You* wouldn't marry a poor man.'

Jordan sighed. 'I would have married you ten years ago, when I thought you were poor.'

'That was when you were young and naïve. When you were a romantic.'

'You think I'm not a romantic any more?'

'How can you be when you're going to marry Stedley? You don't love him, and I know it.'

Jordan didn't like the way this conversation was going. She could cope if they just stuck to sex.

'Could we have a change of subject, please?' she asked tautly. 'I didn't come here to talk about Chad. Whether I love him or not is immaterial. Chad loves me, and he wants to marry me—which is more than I can say for you. All you want is to have sex with me. And kinky sex at that.'

'You call this kinky?'

'Yes. And so was that episode against the window. You've always been kinky, Gino. Making me go without panties and…and doing it to me anywhere and everywhere.'

'You loved it all.'

Oh, why had she brought those things up? Just thinking about them turned her on even more.

Impossible to stay still. Impossible to be patient any longer.

'You're moving,' he chided, taking a firm grip of her hips and forcing her to be still.

'I *want* to move. I'm *going* to move. There! See? I'm moving. And you can't stop me.'

*Stop* her? He didn't want to stop her. Not any longer. He'd wanted to make her wait, to torment her. But he was the one in agony.

His blood pounded in his temples as his body rushed past that point of no return. But she still trembled violently, with undeniable pleasure, crying out in ecstasy.

Damn her, he thought wildly as his own flesh followed. Damn her to hell!

## CHAPTER FOURTEEN

JORDAN came back to consciousness in the four-poster bed, her last recollection being Gino carrying her back there, wrapped in a huge bathtowel. Nothing more. She must have fallen asleep as soon as her head hit the pillow.

The room wasn't dark, Gino having left the bedside lamps on, but he wasn't in the bed. She was alone under the satin sheets. The lights were still on in the sitting room, and she thought she heard a noise coming from there.

'Gino?' she called out as she levered herself up onto one elbow. 'Gino, where are you?'

He materialised in the connecting doorway, a red towel slung low round his hips, the five o'clock shadow on his face giving him a slightly menacing air.

Feeling suddenly vulnerable, Jordan clutched the sheet up over her bare breasts, her actions making his eyes narrow.

'How…how long have I been asleep?' she asked.

'Not long.'

He walked over and sat on the edge of the bed, then reached up to undo the knot on top of her head. Her hair tumbled down over her shoulders. Gino brushed it back with his hands.

'I've been waiting patiently for you to wake up,' he murmured, then bent forward to kiss her on her lips. Lightly at first, and then more hungrily.

As usual, his kisses sent her heartbeat racing and any qualms flying. When he pushed her back onto the pillows and threw the sheet right back off the bottom of the bed she made no attempt to stop him.

But when he reached for the bottle of lotion near the lamp her whole body stiffened.

'What's that for?' she demanded to know.

'Nothing to be alarmed about,' he returned smoothly. 'It says here on the label that this is a love lotion, designed to enhance every sexual activity. It claims aphrodisiacal qualities, an exotic scent and a delicious taste. And, no, before you ask. I didn't buy it. It was here when I arrived, compliments of the management.'

Jordan swallowed when he started unscrewing the lid.

'Don't look so worried.'

'I…I'm not sure I want you to use that stuff on me, Gino.'

He frowned at her. 'Why not?'

'I don't know.' But Jordan *did* know. She was afraid that she might enjoy it too much. That it would make her even more mindless than usual. That she might let him do things she would later regret.

The sudden fear and vulnerability in her eyes touched Gino's conscience. At the same time he refused to back off entirely. This was what she'd come here for, wasn't it?

'Why don't you use it on me, then?'

His suggestion sent her eyes rounding. But not with fear this time. With surprise.

He recalled that he'd always been the boss in the bedroom.

Clearly the idea intrigued her. In actuality, the idea intrigued him, too. He'd never been the passive partner in lovemaking before. Not ever. Who knew? Maybe he'd enjoy it.

'Here—take it,' he said, shoving the bottle into her hands before whisking the towel from his hips.

A downward glance had his eyebrows lifting. He hadn't realised till that moment that he was well on the way to being aroused again.

'I am yours to do with as you will,' he said, and he lay down beside her, his arms bending upwards so that his hands rested behind his head.

Oh, yes, he thought as he felt his flesh

swell even further. He *was* going to enjoy this. Very much so.

Jordan sat up and stared down at Gino's aroused body, not quite sure where she was supposed to start.

In the past she'd reacted only at his command, and never for her own pleasure. The thought of having his entire body at her disposal, however, was sparking an alien feeling of power which was more exciting than she could ever have imagined.

'You won't stop me?' she said, her voice sounding oddly husky.

'I will keep my hands exactly where they are,' he promised.

'You don't look like you need any aphrodisiac lotion,' she told him. 'But you did say that it tasted good, didn't you?'

Jordan's heart started thudding madly in her chest as she knelt up beside him, then tipped the bottle gently sidewards, letting the creamy lotion drip onto him.

He gasped.

'Cold?' she asked cheekily.

'Something like that.'

'I think that's enough,' she said.

'I agree,' he muttered under his breath.

'Now, now—you're not to complain, but to enjoy,' she chided as she put the bottle down on the bedside table. 'This was your idea, remember?'

'Maybe I made a mistake.'

'Not by the look of you.'

He groaned when she bent and licked him with her tongue-tip.

They were right, Jordan thought, somewhat dazedly. It did taste good—somewhere between olives and apples.

Definitely an aphrodisiac as well: it made her want to make love to him with her mouth. All the way.

A wave of heat flushed her skin as she bent her head to him again. First she swirled her tongue around, several times, then she began to slowly take him into her mouth, holding him firmly at the same time with her lotion-slicked hand.

He groaned, and twisted his hips from side to side. But he didn't try to stop her.

Jordan set up a relentless rhythm with her mouth, shocking herself by how much she enjoyed hearing the tortured sounds he began making.

It wasn't till he called out her name that she gave him some respite.

'Is there something wrong, lover?' she asked, as she sat up and pushed her hair back from her flushed face.

'You're treading a fine line there,' he warned her, his breathing ragged. 'I suggest you move on.'

Jordan's eyebrows lifted, his last words bringing a sudden stab of resentment.

*That's what I've been trying to do ever since you left me, Gino. Move on. Yet here I am, in bed with you again. And it's all such an appalling waste of time.*

Jordan's thoughts infuriated her—mostly because she knew she was incapable of walking away right now. She was way too excited.

But perhaps he was right: she wanted him inside her again.

At the same time, she liked the tension she saw in his face. It pleased her to know she could make him suffer, even if it was only physically. She vowed to take her time with him, to make him wait.

'Have to go to the bathroom, lover,' she said. 'Won't be too long. Just lie back and relax.'

Relax!

Gino grimaced when she climbed off the bed and padded her way across the gold carpet.

How could he possibly relax?

He tried some deep, even breathing, his eyes clinging to the bathroom door, willing it to open, desperate for her to come back. But when the door finally opened, and she re-entered the bedroom, she didn't rejoin him on the bed. Instead, she slipped into her high heels and went back into the bathroom.

A minute later she was back, a glass of champagne in her hand, her walk slow and sexy as she undulated towards the bed. As his gaze raked over her Gino's desire to touch was so acute that his hands instinctively began to move.

'Hands behind your head,' she snapped.

Her imperious attitude stunned him, as did the way it turned him on. But even as the blood roared around his veins he longed for that moment when he could take control again— when he could once again show her who was the master here.

'I'm beginning to see that there is more pleasure in taking than receiving,' she purred, a truly wicked smile pulling at her lips.

Any secret hope on Gino's part that she might have come here tonight for reasons other than sex evaporated in the face of that smile.

He swore quietly when she climbed up

onto the bed and straddled him, her high heels still on, the glass of champagne still in her hands. As he stared up at her his level of arousal shot past pleasure, entering the world of near pain.

'Just you wait,' he warned her darkly.

'Now, now. Just be a good boy and keep those hands of yours right where they are.'

His pulse-rate went wild as she remained kneeling above him, holding his stricken gaze as she repeatedly put her finger into the champagne and then into his mouth.

Finally she put the glass down, took him into her hands and pushed him up inside her, not letting him go till he'd been totally enveloped by her body.

Gino moaned at the heat and the moistness of her.

He did not expect her to lean down and kiss him at that stage. That was not what she was here for. But was it the tenderness of her kiss which changed his mind on that score? Or the way she murmured his name against his lips? Whatever—his heart seemed to flower open in his chest, bursting with feelings he'd been trying to suppress.

When he moaned under her mouth, she abruptly terminated the kiss.

'I suppose this is what you want?' she said sharply, and she straightened, her eyes turning wild as she began to move.

He wanted to tell her that, no, it was not what he wanted. But his tortured body had a mind of its own. He struggled to stop himself from coming, not wanting her to see him lose control.

'Total surrender, Gino,' she grated out as she slowed to a more sensual pace. 'That's the name of this game. I know. Because I've been there…done that. You took me there. You don't want to give in…you're afraid that somehow you'll never be the same. And you could be right. I've never been the same. You ruined me for any other man.'

He heard her words, and understood what she was saying. But if he'd ruined her for any other man then she'd ruined *him*. She'd always been there in the back of his mind. Always.

Maybe they didn't love each other any more, but they could—if they gave themselves a chance.

What he had to do was tell her the total truth. How he'd never forgotten her either. How he hadn't run into her by chance. He'd deliberately sought her out.

But no words came from his mouth at that moment. Only raw, naked sounds of desire.

He lasted till she climaxed. After that there was no contest, his back arching from the bed as their bodies shuddered as one.

At some stage he took his aching arms from behind his head. But by then exhaustion had set in. He wanted to hold her, talk to her, but it was a typical case of the spirit being willing but the flesh very weak. When she climbed off him a fog had already begun to descend over his mind. Soon Gino didn't think or feel anything.

Jordan collapsed back on the bed, not moving or speaking till she heard the sound of deep, even breathing. Only then did she steal a glance over at Gino, relieved to see that he was fast asleep.

She still didn't move for a long while, her eyes glistening as she worked out what she was going to do. At last she rose, quietly collecting her clothes from the sitting room and dressing out there. Afterwards she went to the elegant reproduction French writing desk in the corner, and used the gold pen and perfumed paper to write Gino a note.

That done, she carried the note into the bedroom, where she propped it up against a lamp.

After one last tearful glance at his sleeping

face she picked up her shoes and returned to the other room, where she slipped them on, retrieved her purse, and left.

# CHAPTER FIFTEEN

GINO woke to an awareness of light, and of being alone in the bed.

His head and shoulders shot up from the pillow, his eyes darting around the room.

'Jordan?' he called out. 'Where are you?'

No answer.

He jumped out of bed and dashed into the *en suite* bathroom.

Not there.

Not in the sitting room either.

The realisation that she'd gone made him feel sick. Then angry.

She could have waited till the morning—not slunk off like some thief in the night.

He was striding through the bedroom on his way to the toilet when he spotted the folded piece of paper leaning against the lamp base.

Hurrying over, he snatched it up and opened it.

*Dear Gino,*
*I decided to leave this way as I didn't want one of those morning-after scenes. Tonight was great, but there is no future for us. We're just ships passing in the night, just as we were ten years ago. Please do not come after me. You will be wasting your time. I have plans for my future and they do not include you. Go home to Melbourne and marry that Italian girlfriend of yours. She is Italian, isn't she? Of course she is.*
*Ciao. Jordan.*

Gino slumped down on the side of the bed. Shattered did not begin to describe his feelings. Though it was a good start.

He'd made a big mistake not telling Jordan

the truth last night. Hell, he could have at least confessed that he'd broken up with Claudia.

But of course his emotions had been very mixed up last night. So had his intentions. From the moment he'd arrived at that dinner he'd lurched from one train of thought to another.

But his head was clear now. Jordan's leaving him like this had cleared it in a hurry.

He scanned the note again, trying to read between the lines, trying to find some shred of hope that he still had a chance with her.

He couldn't really find any.

Her saying they had no future together reminded him of his deathbed promise to his father. Clearly Jordan wanted marriage, and he simply could not offer her that.

Nothing in that note made him feel good. Nothing except for the bit about his Italian girl-friend. That part sounded somewhat jealous.

Why be jealous if she didn't care?

Gino's heat skipped a beat, but he did not dare to hope too much.

Still, it was all he needed to spark some

action. He could not go to back to Melbourne until he'd explored every avenue. If there was the slightest chance Jordan still cared for him, he was going to grab it.

He didn't know the time, but it had to be quite late in the morning, judging by his extremely bristly chin.

Time to get himself showered, shaved, dressed, and on Jordan's front doorstep.

By mid-morning Jordan was totally sick of herself. She'd been crying on and off since arriving home at some ungodly hour in the morning.

She hadn't slept. Hadn't eaten.

Perhaps if she rang Chad and got that dreadful job over and done with she might feel better.

It was about lunchtime in New York—not the middle of the night or anything.

Feeling simply appalling, Jordan steeled herself for one of the worst phone calls of her life.

When Chad didn't answer straight away, her first emotion was relief. When a woman answered, any relief was swiftly replaced by irritation.

'Can I help you?' the woman said, in a sing-song fashion.

'Could I speak to Chad, please?' Jordan said through gritted teeth.

'Chad, darling. It's for you.'

*Chad darling* finally came on the line.

'Hi there,' he said.

'Chad. It's Jordan.'

'Jordan…'

'Yes, your fiancée,' she bit out. 'Remember me?'

'Ahh.'

'What does that mean?'

'I was going to call you,' he said, in the most guilt-laden voice Jordan had ever heard. And she'd heard quite a few during her lawyering years.

'Who was that woman?' she snapped.

'That was Caroline.'

'Am I supposed to know who Caroline is?'

'I was engaged to her once. Before I came to Australia. We…we had this fight, you see, and I thought… Well, I thought she didn't love me any more…'

'But she does?'

'Yes.'

'And you still love her?'

'Yes, I do. I'm sorry, Jordan.'

Jordan didn't know what to say.

'Look,' Chad went on, 'even before Caroline and I got together again I'd begun to suspect that my proposing to you was a mistake. I mean, men like me…basically, we want a woman who makes being a wife and mother their career. You're a great girl, Jordan. And I really enjoyed our time together. But the truth is you're not what I want in a wife.'

Not what he wanted in a wife.

'You want an American wife?' she said, her voice as deflated as her spirit.

'Yes. That's the bottom line. I want an American wife.'

Like Gino wanted an Italian wife.

'I'm sorry, Jordan,' he added.

Jordan didn't want his apologies. She wanted nothing further to do with him. Ever, ever again.

'About the ring…' he continued.

'What about it?'

'I…er…would you mind sending it to me via international courier as soon as possible? Caroline and I are having an engagement party next weekend.'

Jordan blinked, then shook her head. Why was it that the actions of men would never truly cease to amaze her? 'Sure thing. No trouble. I'll do it first thing tomorrow morning.'

'You're upset with me.'

Gee, how intuitive of you!

'Actually, I'm not, Chad. I'm relieved.'

'Relieved?'

'Yeah. When and if I marry, it will be to a man who really loves me. Bye, Chad.'

She hung up before he could say another single word. Then she sank down onto a nearby chair and wept inconsolably. Not for Chad. But for the fact that no man had ever really loved her or wanted her to be his wife.

All men wanted from her was sex.

By noon she was still curled up in that chair, weeping silent but wretched tears. She was also heartily sick of herself.

'Enough,' she muttered, and headed for the bathroom, and her second shower of the day. The first one had been to rid her of the smell of sex. This one was to wash away her never-ending tears.

She stayed in the shower for ages, tipping her face up into the stream of hot water and letting it cascade down her body. Afterwards she towel-dried her hair, then drew on the pink chenille dressing gown she kept hanging on the back of her bathroom door.

At last she thought she might manage some toast and coffee, and padded her way into her sparkling white kitchen. She'd just turned on the electric kettle and popped two slices of bread in the toaster when her front door buzzer rang.

Jordan froze.

Even before she recovered to walk over and answer her security intercom, she knew who it would be.

'Who is it?' she choked out.

'It's me. Gino.'

Dismay swept in, making her heart sink. 'How did you know where I live?' she demanded to know—before the penny dropped. 'Oh, yes. I forgot. You had me investigated.'

'Let me in, Jordan.'

'I might as well. Because you're not going away, are you?'

'No.'

She pressed the button which would release the lock in the door downstairs, sighing as she turned away and went back to where the kettle had boiled and her toast had popped up.

With a sense of weary resignation, she threw

the toast away, then got another mug down from the cupboard.

She thought about brushing her hair, or putting on some other clothes, but decided not to bother. Let him see her at her worst, with puffy, red-rimmed eyes and not a scrap of make-up on. Then he might take one look and go away.

The knock on her apartment door was loud and firm.

Jordan resashed her robe, then went to answer it.

By the time her hand reached the doorknob, however, there were knots gathering in her stomach. What did he want of her now?

If he'd come for more sex then he was going to be disappointed. He couldn't force her into anything—not now that she and Chad were history.

She breathed deeply several times, then wrenched open the door, adopting a stony mask as her eyes swept over him.

He looked great, she conceded. His eyes

clear, his grooming impeccable, his clothing designed to seduce. There again, he'd always looked sinfully sexy in biker gear. There was something about Gino in tight black jeans and a black leather jacket which would turn any girl's head.

But she was no longer a girl, she reminded herself sternly. She was an adult woman, with a mind of her own.

Time to use it.

'What is it that you want, Gino?' she said sharply. 'I thought my note said it all.'

His eyes searched hers. 'You've been crying,' he returned, with a disarming degree of concern in his face. 'Why?'

'Females cry a lot,' she snapped. 'For all sorts of reasons.'

'You never did when we lived together.'

'I was happy then.'

'And you aren't now?'

The door to a nearby apartment opening made Jordan wince.

'You'd better come inside,' she said quickly, not wanting any of her neighbours to overhear their conversation.

Gino didn't waste any time taking up her offer, she noted, pushing past her into the apartment with his usual confident stride.

Fighting off a sense of doom, Jordan closed the door, then followed him into the open-plan living area.

Gino was impressed with the size and quality of her apartment, but taken aback by the décor. It was so stark! Other than the polished wooden floors, everything was black and white. With no splashes of colour, no photos or pictures on the all-white walls. No knick-knacks on any of the black-lacquered side-tables.

The lounge furniture was black leather and hard-looking, with no big squashy cushions to provide any sense of warmth or comfort. The one rug on the floor was not fluffy and soft underfoot, but serviceable and hard, with a geometric pattern in black and white.

The place was soulless, and cold.

Was that how Jordan thought of herself these days? Was that why she was so unhappy?

Gino was determined to find out. Determined to tell her the truth at last as well.

'Would you like some coffee?' she asked, in a stiffly polite voice. 'I was just about to make some when you showed up.'

He turned round to see that she'd kept her distance, her hands clutching the lapels of her pink dressing gown in a vulnerable gesture which made him feel guilty. So did the evidence of her weeping.

He'd done that to her. Made her afraid. Made her sad.

'Yes, please,' he replied. 'I take it—'

'Black and strong with three sugars,' she finished for him.

His heart turned over. 'You remembered.'

Her eyes suddenly shimmered. 'How could

I forget?' she retorted. 'You practically lived on the damned stuff.'

'I'm Italian. We love our coffee.'

'Don't remind me.'

Gino frowned. 'That I love coffee?'

'That you're Italian!' she snapped, then stormed off into the kitchen, which was visible from the living room. Gino wandered over to sit up at the white breakfast bar, shaking his head when he saw that absolutely everything in the kitchen was white, and very shiny.

'And what does *that* mean?' she said sharply, without turning round from her coffee-making.

'What does what mean?'

'The way you're shaking your head. I can see your reflection in the mirrored splashback.'

Gino didn't doubt it. 'I was wondering why the obsession with white?'

She spun round. Not a good idea when one was holding two full mugs of steaming hot black coffee. But she managed not to spill any.

'White's a very practical colour. Everything goes with it.'

'Everything so long as it's black?'

'Chad loved my place.'

'That says a lot for the man,' Gino shot back, before he suddenly realised something. 'You just said *loved*. Not loves. Would you like to tell me what *that* means?'

Jordan smothered a groan. Trust him to pick up on that. She hadn't meant to tell Gino about Chad. Not unless he'd tried to blackmail her again. But the cat was out of the bag now, so there was no point in trying to lie.

She'd never been a good liar, anyway.

'I rang to break it off with Chad this morning,' she confessed with creditable calm. 'But he got in first.'

'He broke off your engagement?'

'Yes. He discovered that he wanted an American wife after all. Name of Caroline. I gather he spent last night with her.'

'And that's why you've been crying?'

'What do *you* think?'

'I think you're better off not marrying someone who doesn't love you.'

She slanted Gino a reproachful glance as she made her way from the kitchen with the coffee. 'Spoken by an expert on the subject.' She put the mugs down onto the coffee table, then returned to the kitchen for some chocolate biscuits.

'If you were *my* fiancée,' he said, 'I would never look at another woman, let alone sleep with one.'

His words evoked instant fury in Jordan. 'Well, that's not ever likely to happen, is it? My being your fiancée. Look, you had your chance to marry me ten years ago, Gino, and you didn't. You left me and never gave me a second thought till you just happened to run into me again.'

'That's not true,' he denied heatedly. 'Not a day went by when I didn't think of you. Why do you think I never got married? I'll tell you why. Because if I couldn't have you as my wife, I didn't want anyone. That's the bitter truth of it. As for my not coming back for you—I stayed away for ten years because I knew I could never offer you what you deserved. And you're wrong about my running into you by accident last Friday night. That was no bloody accident.'

Jordan just stared at him, her mind spinning at his impassioned declarations. His eyes blazed as they held hers, his hands balled into fists on the counter-top.

'I'd avoided coming to Sydney on business all this time—always delegating and sending someone else when necessary. I knew to keep away from the place. Knew I wouldn't be able to handle being near you. But ten years had gone by. I'd been dating this girl for a while, and my family were pressuring me to marry her. I was getting older, and it seemed ridiculously romantic to let the memory of an affair stop me from marrying and having children of my own. I knew I didn't love Claudia, but I told myself that Italian marriages weren't always a matter of love, but of caring and compatibility. I convinced myself that it would work.'

Jordan was amazed at how much his thoughts and feelings had echoed her own. It had killed her, that trip she'd made to Italy, thinking he was somewhere close but still out of reach.

His eyes begged for understanding as he went on. 'I knew I couldn't do it till I'd made one last trip to Sydney. To see how being in your city would affect me. There's this derelict building site in the middle of Sydney's CBD that Dad bought just before he died, and I hadn't done anything with it. I told my mother that now the time was right to build on it. But really it was just an excuse to come up here and see how I felt. The moment I flew into Mascot that Friday the memories just swamped me, and I knew I couldn't leave without at least finding out what had happened to you. I thought you'd probably be married, a beautiful girl like you. So I was astounded when the PI I hired reported you were a lawyer, and single. More than astounded when I was told where you worked. Hell, I'd been there that very afternoon!

'That near-miss almost sent me crazy. I knew then that I had to see you for myself. So I had you followed when you left work that night. Which was how I came to be down in that bar. It wasn't a coincidence, Jordan. It was all my doing.'

Jordan didn't know what to think. Or feel. He had to be telling her the truth. And yet…

'Why didn't you tell me any of this last Friday night?'

'I wish I had. But I wasn't sure how you felt about me. Or where you were at in your life. I told myself I just wanted to see you again and make sure you were happy. But then we danced and I…I lost my head over you—as usual. Of course there was that little added problem of

my having deceived you ten years ago. I suspected—rightly so—that you weren't going to
be too thrilled with that. And once you were in
my arms I didn't want to take the risk of your
rejecting me. Which you did, Jordan. As soon
as you found out. You rejected me, then
stormed off and accepted another man's
proposal of marriage.'

'You could have told me all this at dinner
last night!' she pointed out, determined not to
take everything he said at face value. She'd
learned from her years of being a lawyer that
people twisted the truth to their own selfish
ends all the time.

'After I found out you were engaged to
another man?' he countered. 'Come on,
Jordan, be reasonable! I have my pride.'

'And I have mine!'

'For pity's sake, can't we get beyond this ridiculous repartee? I've come here to talk to
you. To make you see the truth.'

'The truth is not necessarily the same for different people.'

'Spoken like a lawyer.'

'A lawyer who's sick and tired of being taken for a ride. Your actions speak louder than your words, Gino.'

'My actions brought me here today. I could have flown back to Melbourne this morning and not given you a second thought—as you've just said. But I didn't. I came here to talk to you. The least you can do is give me a hearing.'

'If I must.'

'I'm not leaving till I've said everything that has to be said.'

'In that case, come and have your blasted coffee whilst it's still hot.'

Gino's mouth thinned with frustration as he slid off the stool and walked over to scoop up the mugs from the coffee table.

'What on earth are you doing?' she asked, as she followed him with the plate of biscuits.

'Taking these out onto your balcony. This place gives me the shivers.'

'Huh. You have no sense of style. This is the latest thing in minimalism.'

'How New York! But you're Australian, Jordan. You live in a land of colour and contrasts—of blues, greens, reds and browns. How can you bear to live in this colourless place? At least from your balcony we can see the sparkling blue water and feel the warmth of the sun.'

'How dare you come here and criticise my home!'

'I dare because I care.'

'Since when?' she snapped.

'Since the first moment I saw you. Now, stop arguing with me, woman, and make yourself useful. I can't open that sliding glass door with both my hands full, you know.'

She obeyed blankly, he noted, her face in shock.

For Gino's part, he felt more hopeful than he had since he'd awoken that morning and read that ghastly note. A smile pulled at his mouth as he stepped out through the open doorway.

The balcony was a distinct improvement on the inside, facing east and having privacy walls at each end. Her outdoor furniture wasn't too bad, either, made of a rich red wood. She even had a couple of potted palms in the corners.

The day was pleasantly warm and not too windy, despite it being August. Lots of boats were out on the harbour. Water-lovers always came out in their droves on days like this.

'This is much better,' Gino said, as he put the mugs down on the table and then settled in one of the seats.

His comment seemed to snap her out of her bemused state, and her blue eyes turned cold on him again.

'We'll have to talk quietly,' she said waspishly as she sat down. 'I don't want the neighbours hearing us argue.'

'I have no intention of arguing any more. Have you?'

'Absolutely not!'

'Good. But perhaps we should enjoy our coffee first. Then, if things get a bit heated, we can go back inside.'

Jordan sipped her coffee in silence, whilst Gino gulped his down, then wolfed several of the biscuits. Her appetite had once again disappeared, her emotions in total disarray.

But she was determined not to fall victim to Gino's empty charms. Or to his sudden declaration of caring.

If he cared, then let him show it. And not just in the bedroom.

'I have a proposition to put to you,' he said at last.

'I'm sure you have.'

'No, not that kind of proposition.'

'Then what kind?'

'I want you to come to Melbourne with me

when I go back. I want you to stay with me, at my place.'

Jordan just gaped at him.

'I know you don't believe I really care for you. You've said more than once that all I want from you is sex. I want to prove to you that that's not so. You'll have your own bedroom during your visit. There will be no sex. Just a getting-to-know-each-other-again   process. Then we'll find out if what we feel for each other is love, or just lust.'

'And if it is love?' Jordan choked out. 'What then? You still won't marry me.'

Gino pulled a face. 'We'll cross that bridge when we come to it.'

'I…I don't know, Gino.' She'd promised herself not to give in to what he wanted this time. Promised herself to stay strong.

But what if he did love her as she loved him?

Jordan swallowed, a lump coming into her throat with her finally admitting what she'd been trying to ignore all her life. She did still love Gino. She always had and always would.

Impossible now to walk away. She wasn't that strong.

'All right,' she said quietly, despite being gripped by the fear of having her heart broken even worse this time.

The delight in his face soothed that fear somewhat. 'You mean it? You'll come home with me today?'

'Not today, Gino. I have to go to work tomorrow and sort things out. I have clients, and cases.' And a ring which had to be sent back to Chad.

'Why don't you resign? Good lawyers like you are needed everywhere. You could get a job in Melbourne as easily as Sydney.'

'But I might not be staying in Melbourne,' she pointed out. 'Things might not work out between us.'

'They will.'

She shook her head, not having his confidence. 'Look, I was going to resign anyway,' she admitted. 'Then go overseas for a while. I feel tired, Gino, very tired.'

'Yes, I can see that,' he said.

His gentle tone touched her. As did his soft eyes. 'I…I'm not going to promise anything.'

'You don't have to.'

'If you try to seduce me I'll leave immediately.'

'I won't.'

'A week,' she said at last. 'I'll give you a week.'

'That's not very long.'

'Take it or leave it.'

'I'll take it.'

## CHAPTER SIXTEEN

'So what's up?' Kerry said, as soon as Jordan came out of Frank's office on Monday morning. 'You don't look too happy.'

Jordan had mulled over what she would tell Kerry all night, finally deciding that her friend deserved the truth—or at least an edited version of it.

'Could you get away for a cup of coffee?' she asked her.

Kerry frowned. 'That bad, is it?'

'Not bad. Life-changing.'

Kerry's finely plucked eyebrows arched upwards. 'Life-changing? In what way?'

Jordan scooped in a deep breath, then let it out slowly. 'I've just handed in my resignation.'

'What?' Kerry leapt out of her chair. 'Oh, my goodness, Jordan, *why?*'

'I can't tell you the full reason here.'

'What reason did you give Frank?'

'That Chad had broken our engagement over the weekend and I needed to get away for a while.'

'He didn't!'

'Yes, actually, he did. But if he hadn't I would have. I finally realised that I just didn't love him enough to marry him.'

Kerry grimaced. 'It isn't because of that Italian guy again, is it?'

Jordan didn't know whether to laugh or cry.

Overnight, she'd done her best to feel positive about the possibility of a future with Gino, but deep in her heart she knew things wouldn't work out. He was never going to marry her, and she'd never just live with a man; she was old-fashioned that way.

At the same time, she couldn't see herself marrying any other man—so why not grab what happiness she could whilst it lasted?

'I don't want to say any more till we're away from prying ears and eyes.'

'Okay. I'll just go tell Frank that I'll be away from my desk for a while. I'll say you're upset and I'm taking you downstairs for a cuppa.'

'Good idea,' Jordan said, thinking that wasn't too far from the truth. Handing in her resignation had been one of the hardest things she'd ever done.

Still, Frank had been very understanding, promising to arrange for another lawyer to take over her case-load, which thankfully was minimal at the moment. She'd spent the last few weeks on the Johnson case.

Several minutes later she was sitting over a cappuccino in the café downstairs, with Kerry impatiently waiting for her to elaborate.

'Before you jump to conclusions,' Jordan began. 'I didn't decide not to marry Chad because of a memory. I ran into my Italian again.'

'You ran into him? Where?'

Jordan had already decided not to mention

anything about their original meeting in the Rendezvous Bar.

'At the new client dinner last Saturday night. You seated me right next to him.'

Kerry gaped at her. 'Are you saying Gino Bortelli is your Italian?'

'Yes.'

'Oh, my goodness… But…but he's not a labourer. He's rich and successful! From what I've heard his family's loaded.'

Jordan sighed, then explained what had happened all those years ago.

'I see,' Kerry bit out, not looking too impressed. 'Now I know why you acted so oddly last Saturday night.' Her eyes suddenly widened, as they did when realisation struck. 'You spent the night with him, didn't you?'

'Yes,' Jordan admitted.

'Sunday too, I'll warrant.'

'No. We just talked on Sunday. That's when he asked me to go to Melbourne, and I said I would.'

'Oh, Jordan, don't be such a fool. He used you all those years ago and he'll use you again. Men like him, they change their girlfriends as often as their cars.'

'You're not telling me anything I don't already know, Kerry. But I *have* to do this. I don't have a choice.'

'You love him that much?'

She nodded, tears pricking at her eyes.

Kerry sighed. 'If you ever want to come back, Frank would rehire you in a flash. You know that, don't you? He thinks you're great. We all do.'

'Thank you for saying that. But I won't be back. If things don't work out with Gino I'm going overseas for a while. I might get a job in London. My dad was born in England, so I'm allowed.'

'This is goodbye, then?

Jordan hesitated. She'd never been the kind of girl who kept in touch with old friends. When she moved on, she moved on.

After her original affair with Gino, and then her mother's death, she'd become a loner, through and through.

'I'll keep in touch,' she heard herself say. 'I promise.'

# CHAPTER SEVENTEEN

THE moment he saw her walking through the arrivals gate Gino wanted to rush over and throw his arms around her.

Instead, he just waved, smiled, and walked slowly towards her.

She didn't smile back, her eyes coolish as they flicked over him.

'Hi, there,' he said, whilst privately wondering if she was having second thoughts.

'Hi,' she returned.

'Had a good flight?'

'So-so.'

Gino did his best to ignore her less than joyous attitude. But it wasn't easy.

'I have a car waiting outside,' he said. 'Let's go get your luggage. Do you have much?'

'Just one case. I hope I've brought enough warm things. I nearly died when the pilot said the outside temperature here was twelve degrees.'

His eyes travelled over her black trouser suit, which looked a bit on the thin side. Okay for an office, but not up to Melbourne on a rainy winter's day. 'It is still pretty cold down here, and wet. But my place is temperature-controlled.'

He made small talk with her whilst they waited next to the carousel, asking how her resignation had gone and if there'd been any trouble.

None, apparently.

But her body language remained tense, and negative.

Hopefully, she'd relax once she saw that he'd meant what he'd said about there being no sex this week, just companionship.

Gino had worried that it would be almost impossible for him to keep his hands off her. But nothing was too great a sacrifice, he realised as he stood beside her, if it meant convincing Jordan he was sincere.

'That's mine,' she said, pointing to a medium-sized black bag.

He swept it up with ease, smiling at her as they began to walk towards the exit. 'You do travel light.'

Still she didn't smile, her lovely face taut, her eyes not happy. 'I don't own a lot of clothes.'

'We'll go buy you some nice new things tomorrow. Melbourne is, after all, the fashion capital of Australia.'

'First you criticise my apartment,' she snapped. 'Now my clothes.'

'There's nothing wrong with your clothes,' he lied. 'But black is definitely not your colour.'

'I don't want you to buy me any clothes,' she said firmly.

'Fine. I just thought you might enjoy it. Most women enjoy clothes-shopping—especially when someone else is paying.'

Jordan ground to a halt, her blue eyes flashing at him. 'I am not most women. And I am not your mistress. *Yet.* If and when I agree to such a role in your life, *then* you can tart me up for your pleasure. Till then, you will take me as I am.'

His black eyes flashed back at her. 'I thought I wasn't supposed to take you at all.'

Colour zoomed into her cheeks. 'You know what I mean.'

'I can't say that I do. When I offered to take you clothes-shopping my intention was not to dress you up for my pleasure but to remind you that you are a beautiful woman who looks her best in feminine clothes. You seem to have forgotten that somewhere along the way.'

'I did tell you that I'd changed.'

'Not for the better, it seems.'

'I didn't come all this way to argue with you.'

'No kidding. You were ready for a fight the moment you got off that plane.'

His accusation took Jordan aback. But she quickly realised he was right. Her mental boxing gloves had come up the moment she set eyes on him, looking superb in a sleek grey business suit, with matching overcoat and a scarf slung elegantly around his neck. Suddenly she'd felt dowdy and out of her depth. She'd been more comfortable with the Gino of ten years ago, the one who'd worn jeans and T-shirts and spoken with an Italian accent.

The Gino of today was too slick for her, and too clever by half. He could even out-argue her, which was not an easy thing to do.

'I should not have come,' she said wretchedly.

'Don't be ridiculous. You'll be fine once I get you home and get a couple of glasses of wine into you. I'll even cook you dinner like I used to. Would you like that?'

She blinked, then stared at him. 'You still cook?'

'Not all that often these days. But I will, for you.'

Gino wanted to whoop for joy when she finally smiled.

'Could I pick the meal?'

'Only if you promise to let me take you clothes-shopping tomorrow.'

Her head tipped charmingly to one side, her blue eyes dancing at him. 'The Gino of ten years ago was not as good a negotiator as you.'

'I didn't need to be. Though you took a good bit of persuading at times. You've always had a stubborn streak, Jordan.'

'And you've always had an inflated ego.'

'Good God—she's doing it again. I refuse to talk to you any more, woman,' he said, picking up the suitcase with his right hand and clasping her arm with his left. 'There will be total silence from this moment, till I get you safely in my car and on the way home.'

'You don't need to impress me, Gino,' were her first words after that. He'd just helped into the back of a white limousine.

'There's every need,' he replied. 'I want you to know that you won't lose financially by not marrying Stedley.'

Jordan gave him a startled glance. 'It might have escaped your attention, but I make a very good living as a lawyer. There is no mortgage on my apartment. And I have a very nice car in my garage.'

'But a pathetic wardrobe.'

'Now who's trying to pick a fight?'

Gino grinned. 'I just had to get that in again.'

'What makes you such an expert in female fashion, anyway?'

'I have six sisters.'

'Six!'

'Yep: two older and four younger. They're all clothes-mad. So is my mother. Mum always dragged me along on when she went shopping. Dad refused to go, and she wanted a male opinion she could trust.'

'Why didn't you tell me about your big family all those years ago?' Jordan asked him. 'Why did you let me think your were an only child?'

Gino knew he had to make her understand why he'd lied to her. But it wasn't going to be easy.

'Do you have any idea what it's like being the only son in an Italian household?'

'Not really.'

'I was my father's son and heir—the one who would take over the business when he retired or died. As far back as I remember, my father lectured me on my duty and my responsibility towards the family. If anything happened to him, I was to be the provider and the protector. There was no question about my doing anything else with my life except becoming an engineer, like him. At the same time I was encouraged to hold strong to my Italian roots and culture. That was why I was sent back to the university in Rome. I stayed with an aunt and uncle there till I graduated, living and breathing the Italian way of life. My aunt continually introduced me to Italian girls of suitable marriage age. I'm sure she thought they were all sweet little virgins. But they weren't. Not a single one.'

'I see,' Jordan said, looking thoughtful.

'Don't get me wrong. They were all very nice, very attractive girls. But I didn't fall in love with any of them. I certainly didn't want to marry any of them, although I could have had my pick. By the time I finished my four-year stint over there I was very homesick for Australia, and totally fed up with all things Italian. I might have been born in Rome, but I'd moved to Australia when I was one. Australia was my country and my home. I was also sick of always being introduced as Giovanni Bortelli's son. I never knew if people liked me for myself, or because of my father. When I finally came home, and my father wanted me to go straight into the business with him, I rebelled. I'd had enough, I told him. I needed some space—needed to be free for a while from the pressure of being his son. He reluctantly agreed to give me a year to do just that. Probably because he could see if he didn't I would just take off and never come back. I refused to tell him where I was going, but I did finally tell my mother. Not where I was living, but where I was working.

That's how she knew where to contact me when Dad became ill.'

Gino picked up Jordan's hand within both of his. 'I didn't *mean* to hurt you,' he said sincerely. 'But I know I did. I was just an overgrown boy, Jordan, masquerading as a man. I was selfish and totally self-centred. I like to think I'm a real man now, capable of compassion and caring for others. I won't hurt you again. I promise.'

Jordan wanted to believe him. She *did* believe him, actually. Or she believed his good intentions. But he would hurt her again. History was bound to repeat itself, as it always did.

His Italian family was still a huge obstacle to their finding happiness together, as was that deathbed promise to his father. Gino was never going to go against that promise and marry her.

But none of that seemed to matter when Gino was holding her hand and looking deep into her eyes, the way he was doing right at that moment.

'It's all right, Gino,' she said softly. 'I understand what happened ten years ago. And I forgive you.'

'You've no idea what it means to me to hear you say that.'

'Does your mother know about me?'

'No.'

'Are you going to tell her?'

'Yes.'

'When?'

'Today, if you want me to.'

'No. No, I don't want you to do that. Not yet.'

She turned her head to gaze through the passenger window.

It had begun to rain outside—a soft, gentle drizzle.

'I've never been to Melbourne before,' she said at last.

'You'll like it.'

She turned back to face him. 'How can you be sure?'

He smiled. 'Because I live here.'

She had to laugh. 'You're an arrogant devil.'

'Confident. Not arrogant.'

'What's in a word?'

'You're a lawyer. You should know there's a lot of difference between confident and arrogant.'

'How would you describe me?'

'How many words can I use?'

'As many as you need. What did you think of me the first night we met.'

'Mmm. My first impression was that you were beautiful.'

'Gee, don't get too deep on me.'

Gino grinned. 'The male perspective on first meeting a female is inevitably shallow. It's a hormonal thing. But by the end of the night I knew you were also intelligent, hard-working and kind.'

'Flatterer.'

'I haven't finished. After I moved in with you I swiftly discovered you possessed a unique combination of qualities. Sweetly innocent, yet capable of great sensuality. Strong-willed and stubborn on occasion, but mostly soft and giving. What impressed me the most, however, was your loyalty. I always knew that your love was mine. I never worried that you would ever look at any other man. Not while you were with me.'

His last compliment choked her up. In truth there'd never been another man for her, even after he'd left her. Which was why she was here, sacrificing everything just to be with him.

'And now, Gino? What am I now?'

'You're still you, Jordan,' he said gently. 'Underneath.'

'Underneath what?'

'Underneath the rather formidable façade you've developed over the years. You're still a compassionate, caring woman, Jordan. I could hear that in your voice when you told me about the Johnson case. But being a lawyer has also made you cynical.'

'It's impossible not to become a cynical. The things I've seen, Gino, and heard. People are rotten.'

'No. *Some* people are rotten, Jordan. Lots of people are good. Don't let the minority colour your view of life. I know that that insurance company did the wrong thing by your father. But revenge, whilst temporarily satisfying, can prove to be self-destructive in the long run. Frankly, I think it's high time for you to give the law a break.'

'That's what I'm doing, isn't it?'

'I meant for longer than a week.'

Jordan knew what he meant. He wanted her to stay with him, live with him. Become his *de facto* wife.

But Jordan wanted to be his *real* wife.

'Let's just take one day at a time, Gino.'

'Fine,' he said equably. 'I can do that.'

## CHAPTER EIGHTEEN

'I love your place, Gino.'

Gino glanced up from his cooking with a wry smile on his face.

'You're just saying that.'

'No, no. I mean it.'

'You don't think it's too eclectic? And cluttered?'

'Not at all.'

Jordan could see now why he'd hated her apartment so much.

Gino's penthouse was as far removed from minimalist as one could get. Everywhere there was colour and warmth.

The walls were all painted a soft, creamy yellow, most of the floors were covered in a deep jade-green carpet, and the furniture was a mad mixture of modern and antique—which probably shouldn't have gone together but somehow did. There were cushions of every hue and fabric dotted about the living rooms, plus lots of ornaments, and more photos in frames than she'd ever seen.

The kitchen was huge, and mostly wooden, even the benchtops. A rich wood—probably cedar. The splashbacks were beaten copper, the appliances stainless steel, the floor covered in multicoloured slate. Every imaginable kitchen utensil hung from copper pipes running overhead, put there because Gino said he hated hunting through drawers for things. There was a central island with a sink and a stove, on which Gino was currently cooking the most delicious Bolognese sauce Jordan had ever tasted. He'd cooked it for her every Saturday night during the time they'd lived together.

A secret recipe, he'd once claimed.

Its smell was enough to make anyone's taste-buds water.

'More wine?' Gino asked, putting down his wooden spoon and lifting the bottle of red which he'd opened earlier.

'I shouldn't,' she said, even as she held out her near empty glass.

'Why shouldn't you?'

'You know what I'm like when I drink.'

'That's all right,' he said as he refilled her glass. 'I won't let you have your wicked way with me.'

'You won't?'

'Absolutely not. I meant what I said, Jordan. I need to prove to you that there's more than just sex between us. Hopefully, by Friday, you'll be convinced.'

'Friday? That's not a week. That's only four days.'

He shrugged, then grinned. 'I figured four days was about my limit with you under my roof.'

By Thursday evening, Gino was definitely at his limit.

Not that they hadn't spent a wonderful few

days together. Gino had taken the week off work and spent every waking moment with Jordan. They'd gone shopping together, with Jordan giving in and letting him buy her some lovely feminine clothes. They'd lunched out, but had stayed in each evening, with Jordan very happy for him to cook for her. Afterwards, they'd watched television together, or just sat and talked.

Gino had talked more in the last few days than he had in years, holding back nothing in telling Jordan all about his life and his family.

What he hadn't done was make love to her.

Sleeping had become increasingly difficult each night. Not just because of sexual frustration, but because of the frustration associated with their future together. He wanted to ask Jordan to marry him. But how could he without being tormented? He wished to goodness he'd never made such a stupid promise to his father. But of course he hadn't been thinking clearly at the time.

Now he was trapped in a situation which seemed to have no solution. Not one which Jordan would feel happy with. She was at an age where she wanted marriage and motherhood.

To offer her a *de facto* relationship was a second-rate compromise.

At the same time there was no question of letting her go. Gino had done that once. He was not about to do it again.

He loved this woman. And he wanted her like crazy.

Maybe it was time to stop talking and show her how much.

'I hope this tastes as good as it smells,' Jordan said, as she carried a steaming dish into the dining room.

By Thursday, she'd decided it was her turn to cook.

Cooking was not her forte, but she'd become competent enough over the years, though her repertoire of recipes was limited. She'd sensibly stuck to a tried and true favourite of hers, a Thai-style stir-fry with *hokkien* noodles, and chosen a Margaret River white wine to go with it. She'd even set the dining table, though their other evening meals had been consumed very casually, either at the breakfast bar or in front of the television.

A search of the many kitchen cupboards had uncovered a wide array of place-mats, serviettes, glassware and crockery. She'd chosen yellow placemats and serviettes, plain crystal goblets, and white crockery with yellow flowers on it.

Gino didn't say a word as she put the serving dish onto the mat in the middle of the table—which was not like him at all. Come to think of it, he hadn't sat at the breakfast bar whilst she'd cooked, either, making the excuse that he'd wanted to watch the news on television.

Something wasn't right, Jordan realised with a rush of foreboding. Yet she couldn't think what: they'd been so happy together this week.

'You're very quiet tonight,' she said, as she sat down opposite him and flicked out her serviette.

'Mmm,' came his very uninformative reply, his face remaining pensive as he silently served himself some of the food.

Jordan took a sip of her wine before serving herself a smallish portion, her appetite having suddenly declined.

'What are you thinking about?' she asked, after she'd forced a few mouthfuls down.

Her question seemed to startle him. He frowned as he put his fork down and looked up.

'Us.'

'What about us?'

'I think we should leave this conversation till after we've eaten.'

'I don't agree.'

Gino's eyes hardened a little at her sharp tone. 'Very well. I was thinking how much I love you.'

Jordan's mouth dropped open. As a declaration of love went, this one had been delivered in a less than romantic fashion.

'It's not just lust,' he went on firmly. 'It's love. It's always been love.'

Jordan didn't know what to say. He'd simply dumbfounded her.

'What about you?' he demanded to know. 'How do you feel about me?'

She blinked, then licked her lips. 'I think you know how I feel about you, Gino.'

'I want to hear you say the words.'

'I love you,' she said, her heart turning over at finally giving voice to her feelings. 'I never stopped loving you.'

He groaned, then leapt to his feet, his black eyes instantly ablaze with desire. 'You can't possibly expect me to sit here calmly eating after you've just said that, can you?'

'No,' she choked out, the desire she'd been trying to control all week suddenly breaking free.

He strode round the table, yanked her chair back from the table and scooped her up into his arms.

'There's more I want to say,' he growled as he carried her towards the bedroom. 'More for us to decide. But not right at this moment. I need to make love to you, Jordan. Make love, not have sex. You want that too, don't you?'

'Yes,' she said, emotion flooding her heart. 'Oh, yes.'

Gino cuddled her close to him afterwards, stunned by the passion and the power of their mating. There'd been no foreplay. Nothing but a rapid stripping of their clothes and an immediate fusion of their impatient bodies. It had been all over in seconds, both of them crying out in release together.

'You must know that I *want* to marry you,' he said thickly, his lips buried in her hair. 'But I can't.'

'I know,' she said sadly.

'It isn't right,' he said with a groan. 'I want you to be my wife.'

* * *

Jordan heard the pain in his voice, and knew she had to do something.

She cupped his cheeks with her hands and lifted his head so that their eyes could meet.

'I will *be* your wife,' she said. 'In every way that counts. I will love you and look after you and have your children, if that's what you want.'

His eyes widened. 'You'd have my children? Even though I can't give them my name?'

'There's no reason why I can't take your name, Gino. That's a simple matter of changing it by deed poll. All we'll be missing is a piece of paper. Our love is stronger than that, surely?'

Jordan was shocked when his eyes started glistening. 'You are a truly wonderful woman.'

'An ordinary woman, in love with a truly wonderful man. We can make things work if we love each other enough, Gino.'

'Yes. Yes, you're right.'

Still he didn't look totally happy.

'I suppose you're worried about your

mother,' Jordan said. 'And your six sisters. You're worried what they'll think.'

'They'll get used to the idea.'

Jordan suspected that Gino's family would look askance at their relationship for ever. It was not the Italian way to live together without the blessing of the church.

But that was just too bad.

'When are you going to tell them?' she asked.

'Tomorrow. After we've gone ring-shopping.'

'Ring-shopping?'

'Just because we won't have that piece of paper it doesn't mean we can't have proper rings.'

'Rings, as in plural?'

'Of course. An engagement ring and a wedding ring for you. And a wedding ring for me. I want everyone to know that I'm taken.'

Jordan struggled to hold back her tears. 'I'd like that.'

He smiled. 'I thought you might.'

# CHAPTER NINETEEN

'HAPPY with those?' Gino asked as they emerged from the jeweller's into Collins Street.

'They're lovely,' Jordan replied, not able to take her eyes off her engagement ring. It was absolutely stunning, yet very simple. A single brilliant-cut diamond set in white gold, with two smaller baguette diamonds on the shoulder settings. The wedding band next to it was even simpler. Just a narrow white gold band.

Gino's ring, by contrast, was wider, and made in yellow gold, with small diamonds set at regular intervals around the whole circumference. It suited his more flamboyant style, she thought.

They were walking slowly back to where Gino had parked his car when his cellphone rang.

Jordan stood there in the watery sunshine, admiring her rings whilst Gino answered it.

'I did tell you I didn't like their scaffolding,' Gino muttered irritably at one stage. 'No. No, I need to see this for myself. I'll be there in about twenty minutes. Problems at work,' he said to Jordan as he put the phone back into his trouser pocket. 'No point in trying to explain it. Look, I could be there for a couple of hours. I'll drop you off home first. What time is it now? Half-past twelve. I shouldn't be any later than three in getting back. Possibly four. You can catch up on your beauty sleep. You didn't get much last night,' he added, with a wicked gleam in his eye.

'You didn't, either.'

'I got more than I did the last few nights, I can tell you.'

'Are we still going to visit your mother tonight?'

'Absolutely. I'll ring her from work and line up something.'

Jordan felt her stomach tighten. 'Maybe she won't want to see me.'

'Don't cross your bridges till you come to them, Jordan.'

By three p.m., Jordan found herself clock-watching. Nerves over the evening ahead had meant she'd been incapable of settling to anything. And sleeping had been out of the question.

By four, her agitation was beyond bearing.

She didn't like to call Gino on his cellphone. He'd promised to be home as soon as he could. But he'd left the number with her, and it seemed silly to stew when a simple call would soothe her mind.

Picking up Gino's home phone, she punched in his number and waited for him to answer.

His phone rang a few times, then switched to his voicemail, which said that he couldn't come to the phone right now, but to leave a message and he'd get back as soon as he could.

Jordan hesitated, then hung up, thinking that he was probably driving home at this very moment.

Ten minutes later she wished she'd left a message. Gino still wasn't home. She was just about to call his number again when the phone rang. With a rush of relief, she hurried over and swept up the receiver.

'Gino?' she said.

'Is that Jordan?' a female voice asked—a voice with a distinct Italian accent.

'Er…yes.'

'This is Maria Bortelli. Gino's mother.'

'Oh…' Jordan didn't know what to say. Had Gino dropped in to see his mother before coming home? If so, then why wasn't it Gino on the phone?

She didn't like the sound of this.

'I knew Gino would want me to ring you. He called me and told me about you.'

'I see,' Jordan said. 'You're…not upset with me, are you?' Certainly she sounded upset.

'Upset with you? No, no. Not with you. Or Gino. That is not why I am calling. There has been an accident, Jordan. At one of Gino's building sites.'

Jordan's heart jumped into her mouth.

'What kind of accident? Dear God, please tell me Gino's alive. Tell me he's all right.'

'He has had a nasty fall. Some scaffolding gave way under him. The doctors are doing tests on him right now. His hard hat was knocked off in the fall.'

'Is he conscious?'

'No.'

A tortured cry escaped Jordan's lips. If Gino died, what would she do? He was her life now, her reason for living.

'You should come,' Mrs Bortelli said. 'Gino would want you to be here. With him.'

'Yes, yes,' Jordan said, her heart thudding wildly in her chest. 'I'll catch a taxi. Just tell me where to go.'

The ride to the hospital felt endless, the roads choked with Friday afternoon traffic. The taxi dropped her off at the entrance, and Jordan rushed through the glass doors, her eyes already searching for the lifts. Mrs Bortelli had told her what floor to go to, and what ward.

Finally she spotted the lifts, over in a far corner of the foyer.

As she hurried over, Jordan could not help noticing a woman standing by the lift doors, staring at her. She was in her late fifties, perhaps, an elegantly dressed lady, with wavy dark brown hair and even darker eyes.

'Jordan?' she said.

'Yes?'

'I am Maria Bortelli.' Her dark eyes swept over her, her warm smile coming as a surprise. 'You are as beautiful as Gino said.'

Jordan was so taken aback she didn't know what to say.

'Come,' Mrs Bortelli went on, and took Jordan's arm. 'They have taken Gino up for surgery, so he is now on a different floor to the one I told you.'

'Surgery! What kind of surgery?'

'Brain surgery. There is some bleeding which has to be stopped.'

When Jordan swayed, Mrs Bortelli held her steady.

'*Si, si*—I know how you feel,' she said gently. 'I felt the same way when they first told me. But I keep telling myself not to worry. My Gino is strong, and he is in good hands. I have been down here in the hospital chapel, praying for him.'

Jordan had never been a big one for prayer. She'd always believed that God helped those who helped themselves. But she suspected she was about to get acquainted with the practice.

'Did my son buy you those rings?' Mrs Bortelli asked during the ride up in the lift.

Jordan lifted her hand to stare blankly down at her engagement and wedding rings.

'Yes,' she choked out. 'This morning.'

How happy they had been! And now…

'Gino told me about the promise he made to his papa.'

'He did?'

'It was foolish of him.'

'He knows that now. But he won't dishonour it.'

Mrs Bortelli shook her head. 'He is a good son. But it is not right to expect you not to have a real marriage. Still, we will just have to make the best of it. He loves you, and refuses to marry any other girl.'

The lift doors opened and the two women stepped out into the wide corridor, with its familiar hospital smell of polish and disinfectant.

'You don't mind that I'm not an Italian girl?' Jordan said.

'Why should I mind?'

'Gino's father obviously minded.'

'Giovanni was much older than me, and old-fashioned. Ours was an arranged marriage, not a love-match. I promised myself that my children would only ever marry for love. That is one promise *I* will never dishonour. Love is far more important than a piece of paper.'

'I'm so glad you feel that way.'

When his mother smiled, Jordan could see where Gino got his looks and his charm.

'You and Gino will make beautiful children together.'

'If we get the chance,' Jordan said, her emotions suddenly catching up with her again. 'Oh, Mrs Bortelli,' she cried, tears flooding her eyes, then spilling over down her cheeks. 'I love him so much.'

'I can see that, my dear. Come,' she said, and linked arms with Jordan. 'He won't be out of surgery for some time. We will go back down to the hospital chapel and pray some more.'

Gino knew he was dreaming. It had to be a dream. Because he and Jordan had just been married, in an old church he did not recognise. Jordan looked like an angel dressed in white, a beautiful Botticelli angel. She beamed up at him as they walked arm in arm back down the aisle out into bright sunshine.

Not Melbourne, he realised as his eyes looked down the ancient stone steps upon a city which he recognised.

They were in Rome.

That was it, Gino realised in his dream. That was the way. Why hadn't he thought of it before?

He struggled to wake up. But he couldn't seem to shrug off the blanket of sleep which was imprisoning his body. Why couldn't he wake up? he thought frustratedly. What was wrong with him?

The nurse in Recovery assigned to Gino was watching him carefully.

'You shouldn't be waking up yet,' she said, when his eyelids started fluttering wildly.

When he began muttering, and trying to lift his head, she put gentle but firm hands on his shoulders.

'Lie still,' she whispered. 'Everything went fine in the operation. But you must rest some more.'

His eyelids shot open, frightening the life out of her.

'Jordan,' he choked out.

'You want me to tell Jordan you are all right?'

He shook his head from side to side.

'Tell her. Tell her there is a way,' he said, then promptly fell back to sleep again.

And rightly so. He shouldn't be coming round for quite a while yet.

Just then Dr Shelton strode in, and the nurse was relieved that his patient was no longer thrashing about. As the doctor checked his patient's vital signs, the nurse explained what had happened.

Dr Shelton frowned.

'Amazing,' he said. 'He shouldn't be coming round for at least another half-hour or so. Jordan, did you say?'

'Yes.'

'Man or woman?'

'He didn't say. But my guess is a woman.'

The doctor's smile was wry. 'That would be my guess, too.'

Jordan sat in the waiting room, surrounded by the other women in Gino's life. His six sisters had descended at various intervals during the last couple of hours, all very anxious about their beloved brother.

Jordan had been touched by their love and concern, and totally overwhelmed by their warm acceptance of her. None of Gino's sisters made her feel like an interloper, or resented her not being of Italian heritage. They'd been a little surprised, but also fascinated, when she'd told them about her affair with Gino all those years ago. His youngest sister, Sophia, had thought it the most romantic story she'd ever heard. They'd all echoed their mother's opinion that it had been very foolish of Gino to make that promise to his father.

But they all knew that their brother would not break his promise.

Telling them her story had distracted everyone from the seriousness of the moment. But now the story had been told, and they'd all suddenly fallen silent.

As if on cue, a doctor dressed in surgical greens entered the room. He was a tall, slim man, in his late forties, perhaps, with a long face, a receding hairline and intelligent blue eyes.

Mrs Bortelli immediately jumped up and rushed over him.

'Is my son going to be all right, Doctor?' she asked.

He took both her hands in his, smiling as he patted them.

'He's going to be fine,' he said, to a collective sigh of relief from the sisters.

Jordan, however, just closed her eyes and thanked God for answering her prayers.

'We stopped the bleeding and flushed out the old blood. The scan shows his brain is looking totally undamaged. He's still out of it, but should be awake and back in his bed within an hour. Now, is there a lady here called Jordan?'

Jordan bolted to her feet. 'That's me.'

'I have a message for you from my patient.'

'A message? But…but…how?'

'He came round for a few seconds and asked the nurse to tell you there is a way. Does that make any sense to you?'

'Yes,' she choked out, nodding and crying at the same time. 'Yes, it makes perfect sense.'

# CHAPTER TWENTY

JORDAN emerged into the late-afternoon sunshine, Gino's arm hooked through hers.

"I never thought I would see this day," she said to him. 'Oh, Gino, I'm so happy I could burst.'

'Happiness becomes you.' He leant over to kiss her glowing cheek. 'So does white.'

She turned her smiling face and kissed him back on the mouth.

After a full thirty seconds, the photographer cleared his throat very noisily. The happy couple broke apart, the bride blushing, the groom beaming.

'I need the entire wedding party, please?' the photographer commanded, as he waved his arms about with theatrical panache. He was

Italian, but spoke English very well, having spent some years in England.

'That's the only drawback with Italian weddings,' Gino muttered under his breath as everyone tried to assemble on the old church steps. 'Sometimes they make *Ben Hur* look like a small production.'

'I know what you mean,' Jordan returned, with a little laugh.

Aside from the bride and groom, the wedding party had six bridesmaids, six groomsmen, five small pageboys and seven little flower-girls. And that didn't count the mother of the groom and Gino's uncle Stefano, who'd kindly given Jordan away.

'If we'd had this wedding in Melbourne it would have been even bigger,' Gino told her. 'Probably two or three hundred guests. Today we only have a hundred.'

'Speaking of guests, thank you so much for flying Kerry and Ben over,' Jordan said, waving to her friend and her fiancé. 'It was very generous of you.'

'Couldn't have everyone sitting on my side of the church now, could I?'

'No more talking, please,' ordered the photographer. 'Just smile!'

They all smiled whilst he clicked away for ages. Finally he stopped, after which Jordan was besieged by every single male guest, wanting a kiss from the bride.

'Enough!' Gino said at long last, and shepherded Jordan down the steep steps to the waiting limousine which would whisk them off to the reception venue—a lovely villa overlooking the River Tiber. More photographs were scheduled to be taken in the lush gardens, which featured some simply amazing fountains.

'It's so good to have my beautiful bride to myself,' Gino said with a possessive clinch once they were alone in the back of the limousine. 'My beautiful *Italian* bride.'

'Not quite yet,' she returned. 'We have to wait six months to apply for spousal citizenship.'

'That's just another piece of paper,' Gino said. 'You are already Italian in spirit. Everyone says so.'

Jordan smiled. 'I simply adore Italy. And Italians. All your family make me feel so loved.'

'You are a very lovable woman,' Gino said, and kissed her softly on the cheek.

Jordan's heart turned over. 'You haven't told me where you're taking me on our honeymoon,' she whispered.

'We will stay tonight in Rome, then tomorrow we are going to set sail on a cruise through the Mediterranean on a luxury yacht. I hope that is to your liking?'

'Anywhere with you is to my liking, Gino.'

Gino smiled at the woman he loved more than life itself. 'You are going to make the most beautiful mother.'

'Yes,' she returned, her lovely blue eyes twinkling with sudden mischief. 'In about eight months' time.'

Gino's breath caught. 'You're pregnant already?' She'd only stopped taking the pill last month.

'It's not really a surprise, is it? You never leave me alone.'

'You don't mind become a mother this soon?'

'Are you kidding me? I'm nearly thirty years old. It's way past time, don't you think?'

"It is the right time,' he said. 'Ten years ago would not have been the right time, Jordan. I would not have made a good father then. I will be a good father to our children now: more patient, and less selfish.'

'I needed to grow up too,' she conceded. 'And to do what I had to do. But I think I've had my fill of being a legal crusader now. I want to live a more peaceful life as a wife and mother.'

Gino's laugh took her aback.

'What does that laugh mean?'

'Who are you kidding, Jordan? You were born to be a lawyer—just as I was born to be an engineer. I bucked my destiny for a while, but I actually love building things—just like you love getting justice for your clients. You'll soon become bored with being just a wife and mother.'

'You think so?' Admittedly, there had been times in the last few months when she'd missed the cut and thrust of the court room, the adrenaline rush she got when she heard that the jury had reached its verdict, and she missed the kind of satisfaction she got from winning cases like Sharni Johnson's.

'I *know* so,' Gino said. 'Look, when we finally return to Melbourne, why not open your own practice? Then you can work your own hours and pick only the clients you really care about.'

Jordan smiled. 'You know me too well.'

'Indeed I do,' he said, with that knowing gleam in his eyes. 'So, my love, what are you wearing underneath that gorgeous wedding dress of yours?'

'That's for me to know and you *not* to find out,' she retorted saucily. 'Not till tonight.'

He peered deep into her eyes till she blushed. 'I think I know already.'

'You're a wicked man,' came her shaky admission. 'You make me do wicked things.'

'You love it.'

'I love *you*.'

Gino sighed a triumphant sigh. 'I will never tire of hearing you say that.'

'I love you,' she repeated, her eyes sparkling as she lifted her mouth to his.

# MILLS & BOON PUBLISH EIGHT LARGE PRINT TITLES A MONTH. THESE ARE THE EIGHT TITLES FOR JANUARY 2008.

———————— ❧ ————————

**BLACKMAILED INTO THE ITALIAN'S BED**
Miranda Lee

**THE GREEK TYCOON'S PREGNANT WIFE**
Anne Mather

**INNOCENT ON HER WEDDING NIGHT**
Sara Craven

**THE SPANISH DUKE'S VIRGIN BRIDE**
Chantelle Shaw

**PROMOTED: NANNY TO WIFE**
Margaret Way

**NEEDED: HER MR RIGHT**
Barbara Hannay

**OUTBACK BOSS, CITY BRIDE**
Jessica Hart

**THE BRIDAL CONTRACT**
Susan Fox

 MILLS & BOON
*Pure reading pleasure*

1207 Rom LP

# MILLS & BOON PUBLISH EIGHT LARGE PRINT TITLES A MONTH. THESE ARE THE EIGHT TITLES FOR FEBRUARY 2008.

---

## THE GREEK TYCOON'S VIRGIN WIFE
Helen Bianchin

## ITALIAN BOSS, HOUSEKEEPER BRIDE
Sharon Kendrick

## VIRGIN BOUGHT AND PAID FOR
Robyn Donald

## THE ITALIAN BILLIONAIRE'S SECRET LOVE-CHILD
Cathy Williams

## THE MEDITERRANEAN REBEL'S BRIDE
Lucy Gordon

## FOUND: HER LONG-LOST HUSBAND
Jackie Braun

## THE DUKE'S BABY
Rebecca Winters

## MILLIONAIRE TO THE RESCUE
Ally Blake

MILLS & BOON®
*Pure reading pleasure*

0108 Rom